TO PENNY AND BRIDGET — AGAIN

VIKING
Published by the Penguin Group
Penguin Books USA Inc., 375 Hudson Street, New York, New York 10014, U.S.A.
Penguin Books Ltd, 27 Wrights Lane, London W8 5TZ, England
Penguin Books Australia Ltd, Ringwood, Victoria, Australia
Penguin Books Canada Ltd, 10 Alcorn Avenue, Toronto, Ontario, Canada M4V 3B2
Penguin Books (N.Z.) Ltd, 182–190 Wairau Road, Auckland 10, New Zealand

Penguin Books Ltd, Registered Offices: Harmondsworth, Middlesex, England

First published in 1995 by Viking, a division of Penguin Books USA Inc.

1 3 5 7 9 10 8 6 4 2

LIBRARY OF CONGRESS CATALOGING-IN-PUBLICATION DATA
Mahy, Margaret.
The other side of silence / Margaret Mahy.   p.   cm.
Summary: As a member of a gifted, idiosyncratic, and argumentative family,
twelve-year-old Hero chooses mutism until she reconciles the true with the real in her life.
ISBN 0-670-86455-2
[1. Mutism, Elective—Fiction. 2. Self-realization—Fiction.
3. Family problems—Fiction.] I. Title.
PZ7. M27730t 1995 [Fic]—dc20 95-8615 CIP AC

A Vanessa Hamilton Book

Printed in USA
Set in Trump Mediaeval

—Contents—

— PART ONE —

True Life

I can't remember the first time I heard the scream, but I know I did hear it from time to time as I scrambled from one tree to another in the forest around Squintum's House. It was always faint and far away. I could never work out just what bird it was, screaming like that, and often I couldn't work out if I was really hearing it at all.

I had better put down that, back then when I was twelve, I never screamed myself. Well, I almost never spoke. I had somehow magicked myself into silence. All the same, even in the heart of my silence, I was still a word child.

And I had better explain that, back then when I was only twelve, I had two lives. The life I lived with my family was my *real* life, but the *tree* life—the early-morning life, which I lived before anyone else was up and about—was also my *true* life even though it was partly invented. Real life is what you are supposed to watch out for, but an invented life, lived truly, can be just as dangerous.

Every morning I would leave our house and go down the road toward a park . . . not that I spent much time *there*. For along one corner of the park was a wall, and on the other side of the wall was the old Credence house, and the house stood in the middle of a forest.

The rates were so high in our suburb, Benallan, that many of the larger gardens had been subdivided. But the Credence house was just as it had always been. It looked like a house in a storybook.

In front of it spread the forest, full of trees that had been planted on purpose, and many other accidental ones . . . seedling sycamores and wild plum. And I would go over the park wall into the trees, and climb up and down—backward and forward, branch to branch—across the ruined garden below. Only the birds knew where I was—well, birds *and* the house itself—the Credence house, watching me from one particular high white window—a milky eye.

Occasionally I heard a thin cry—well, I thought I heard it. It always melted into nothing, as my ear was trying to take charge of it. Mostly there was no noise except the sound of the city breathing steadily, somewhere beyond the trees. This breathing didn't break the early-morning silence; it only seemed to deepen it.

And after I had been climbing for a while, I would hear, morning after morning, the snap of a closing door and, far below me, something would move purposefully out into the garden. Looking down through the outstretched branches, I would see the owner of the forest, Miss Credence herself, testing the day. She would pause to pull out a weed here, a weed there—going through the movements but not meaning to do any real gardening. She always wore a long black cloak, and a black hat, the wide, bent brim hiding her face from anyone looking at her from above. Sometimes, smoke curled out from under the brim because, when she was in the garden, she smoked what looked to me like cigars, and so she seemed to be an entirely different person from the Miss Credence I used to see behind the counter in the Benallan post shop, which was what we had to call post offices these days. In the post shop she wore twinsets of powder blue or moss green, and a silver locket on a chain, telling any careless smokers that her post shop was smoke-free. But here, in the early morning, walking dreamily along winding overgrown paths, she always wore the black cloak and trailed a veil of smoke behind her. She swung a basket as she strolled, and rarely looked up into the trees. But even if she had glanced upward, I somehow imagined she wouldn't have been able to see *me*. Miss Credence lived in a different space from the marvelous child I became every morning, dancing between sky and garden. The ground, and everything that went on directly below me, might belong to her, but I was . . . I had imagined myself into being . . . a spirit of leaves and air.

All the same, once Miss Credence appeared, the whole forest would begin to tremble and thrill with waiting birds . . . sparrows, starlings, blackbirds, and thrushes. Ducks came waddling at speed from the creek that ran behind her house and under the wall out into the park, quacking as they came. After patrolling her forest, Miss Credence would reach a space in the trees. Plunging her hand into the basket she would throw out handfuls of bread in all directions. A rapid thud-thud-thud of wings! Within seconds she would be ankle deep in a living carpet of sparrows, pecking like toys wound up to go; all so used to being fed each morning that they flew down at once, instead of closing in cautiously, branch by branch, watching out for cats, as they did at our house. Starlings and blackbirds were so bold that they perched on Miss Credence's shoulders, or on her hat, even landing directly in her basket. Once the bread had been thrown out she would stand completely still, while, up in the trees, I would grow still too. At last she would turn and retreat, birds following her right to her front door. Then I would finish my early-morning journey.

As the trees had grown into each other, I could move from one side of Credence land to the other without once setting foot on earth. At some points in my journey I would be close to the house, on a level with its tower, and could see it quite clearly. It sat in the middle of a narrow, curving, shaggy meadow . . . a lawn gone wild. A wide fringe of sprawling leaves and tall dry stems, which had once been a garden, stretched around it, and overgrown daisy bushes billowed out on either side of the front door. Miss Credence slipped in and out of this door, edging between the daisies, like something wild coming out of its hole. Something fabulous. As for me, I found it easy to convince myself I was more than a trespassing climber. Once I was up in the trees I turned into the true child of the wild woods, someone who had been fostered and fed by birds.

Real Life

I have already said that, though I didn't talk, I was a word child. But in my family we were all word people. Words had recently swept us to Benallan. And these powerful words were those written down by my mother. Annie had theories about bringing up wonderful, talented children, and, since the beginning of the year, had lectured in the Education Department of the university.

"I never thought I'd find myself living in a trendy suburb,"

Annie sometimes said. "Are we turning into yuppies?"

"You are," Athol, my brother, replied. "You've got a personalized number plate. RAPPER 1!"

"It was a *present*," cried Annie. "We *have* to use it or Rappie would be hurt." Rappie, my Rapper grandmother, had actually given that number plate to my father, Mike, but it was Annie who mostly drove the Peugeot (our best car since the great family car crash three years ago).

"Put the number plate on the Volkswagen," suggested Athol. "That would cancel the yup."

"Cancel the yup, but concentrate the Rap attack," Annie replied.

Rappie declared Benallan was filled with snobs, but when she was talking to people outside the family she always managed to let them know that her son had recently moved there, and owned a Peugeot. I'm sure, though, she never once told them that it was Annie who earned the money that had paid for our new house.

"But isn't it great being so close to the university?" Annie asked Athol in a wheedling voice. "We can walk there in ten minutes."

"You don't, though," said Athol. "Walk, I mean!"

"I always have to carry so many books," Annie pointed out, which was quite true. "Nobody ever realizes how strong bookish people have to be, just to get from place to place."

Supposing *I* had been turned into a book back then I would have wanted to turn into *The Jungle Book*, the story of Mowgli, a boy who lived in the jungle and talked the language of the animals. Or I might just have made do with *The Secret Garden*. But

I would probably have turned into *Old Fairy Tales*, which was the book everyone read to me when I was small—the book I used for secret advice . . . for divination. Even when I was as old as ten or eleven, I would try to take *Old Fairy Tales* by surprise, opening it anywhere, pointing with the first finger of my left hand (my fortune-telling finger) and taking advice from the line I found myself pointing at. *On your life, give no answer*, I once read. And, *If you will not tell me anything, tell your sorrows to the old stove in the corner.*

Ginevra and Athol, my older sister and brother, would never have found their fortunes in *Old Fairy Tales*. Ginevra's fortune might have been printed out by the spirits that live in computers. "You have hacked your way into the heart of the universe," they would suddenly tell her, the words appearing out of nowhere and marching across the blue screen.

And I'm still not too sure about Athol. Once I checked up, pointing to a line in a book that he had left open on the arm of a chair. *Is it possible,* the book asked me, *that there is another shadow universe which we can only detect through gravitational effects?* It was easy to believe Athol lived in a shadow universe, even though he showed up for breakfast every morning, looking ordinary enough. As for my little sister Sap, well, at the time I'm writing about she carried her book with her. She was *armed* with it. It was edited by a woman called Josepha Heifetz Byrne and was called *Mrs. Byrne's Dictionary of Unusual, Obscure and Preposterous Words.* Back then, Sap (short for Sapphira, which gives you a clue about my parents) would sometimes choose a word and find ways of using it. "What a collieshangle!" she used to say, smirking around the room.

"Don't be a cogger!" It grew so irritating that even Mike stopped asking Sap what each new, preposterous word meant, and she'd stand there, longing to be questioned. "I'm working my way through the letter *C*," she'd cry, and after a bit, she'd tell us what the word meant, whether we wanted to hear or not. Mind you, I used to look up some of the words afterward, and so did Athol. Mrs. Byrne says a *cogger* is a false flatterer, so it must have been a hard word for Sap to bring into any conversation because there wasn't a lot of false flattery in our family.

In fairy tales girls and boys leave their homes in mills or castles or hovels or whatever, and set off into forests where they find wonders. It is dangerous, in there among the trees, but amazing things happen to fairy-tale children. Through the forces of wickedness, they are abandoned and lost. Through good luck, or because of their kind hearts, they are discovered, or even discover themselves, and marry princes and princesses. Or perhaps these lost children become children of the forest, and learn its secret roadways. (The Bandar-log, the monkey tribe of *The Jungle Book*, had roads and cross roads, up hills and down, laid out as high as a hundred feet above the ground—that's what the story says, anyway. And when they carried off Mowgli, a boy who had been found and cared for by wolves, he couldn't help enjoying the wild rush through the trees, though the terrible check and jerk at the end of the swing brought his heart between his teeth.)

When we moved into our Benallan house, Ginevra had already left home, and there was no more yelling and slamming of doors. She had written off our pre-Peugeot best car, a Fiat, walking away from the crash unhurt except for a few bruises, and had then vanished, shouting as she went that she would have her revenge. ("What for?" Mike had called after her. "It doesn't matter. I'll have it," she cried. And those were the last words we had heard her say.) Her revenge had been to go to Australia. Cards with Australian stamps on them came quite regularly once a week, all declaring that she was well and making pots of money. There was never any address to write to. And the postmarks were never the same, two weeks running. ("Well, at least she isn't holed up in King's Cross," said Athol, looking at a postcard that had come from somewhere in Queensland.)

The new house seemed open and sunny—sometimes silent, too. Annie, a great talker, was often away lecturing, or attending some conference or other. Athol, who was finishing an M.A. degree, worked for hours on end in the little room we used for an office in those days. Or he sat hunched at the sunny end of the table, peering over the top of some book and smiling his Cheshire cat smile, light reflecting off his glasses. Mike did all the housework. He *said* he enjoyed it, but this was one of the things that infuriated Rappie. She visited us most days, sometimes jogging across the park and turning up for breakfast.

"Why don't *you* go out and find a job for yourself now the children are older?" I heard her ask him as he brought her some cornflakes. "Athol could easily keep an eye on Hero and Sap after school."

"Mum," Mike replied, "why don't you believe me when I tell you I quite *like* running a house? And, besides, I want to be here when Sap and Hero come home from school."

"Yes, well, of course, Hero has Problems," said Rappie, somehow managing to give the word *problems* a capital *P.* "And you know who I blame, don't you?" She thought my silence was Annie's fault . . . a punishment for my mother's pride, as well as for her frequent absences.

Once our old furniture was set up in the new house, once the cats, Windcheater and Motley, had grown relaxed enough to be allowed out into the new garden, and we had managed to get the washing machine into the laundry by taking off the door, we began to explore the Benallan streets. Mike took Sap and me along Edwin Street (our street that is) into Benallan Drive. Half a block along Benallan Drive, we would swoop into Credence Crescent, then veer off along Park Place. Park Place may be one of the great properties on the Monopoly board, but Benallan's Park Place is just about two houses long . . . houses with big gardens, that is. NO EXIT, says the sign at the beginning of the lane, and at the end, past other signs forbidding dogs and motorbikes, you can see a children's playground. I wasn't too crazy about playgrounds, but early in the morning or in the evening, as long as I was on my own, I enjoyed the swings. Swinging seemed to be as close as I would ever get to flying.

As we walked toward the park gates, the high wall that separated the Credence garden from the rest of Benallan rose on the left. Over the years, idealistic students had sprayed messages all over this wall—NO NUKES FOR NZ and SUPPORT GAY RIGHTS, and so on. Trees leaned over from the Credence side, dropping leaves all over the footpath, so I realized straightaway that there was a forest behind the wall. A house, too, of course, and a woman who lived in the house. Her father had written on philosophy, and had once been vice-chancellor of the university. But the only living Credence worked at the Benallan post shop, selling stamps and weighing parcels. Not that the house and the woman seemed important to me in the beginning. It was only the forest that mattered.

Time and time again, when I was on the swings, I would try to work myself up high enough to stare down, for a second, into that forest, but all I ever saw were trees, trees, trees, crowding up against the wall, like dangerous prisoners planning to break out and take over the city.

After a week or two in Benallan, I began going off on my own. I'd write down where I planned to go on the blackboard that Mike had tacked on to the kitchen wall beside the fridge, and take off really early in the morning to do my swinging before mothers started bringing little kids into the playground. Up in the air . . . wheeeeeee! Sure enough, just like it says in *The Jungle Book*, there was a check, a hesitation, at the end of the swing which . . . well, it brought my heart between my teeth all right, though it didn't frighten me exactly. Well, it *half* frightened me, I suppose, but it thrilled me, too. I felt that if I was ever brave enough to let go, I might fly over the wall, changing into something wonderful as I flew.

Well, of course I never let go, but at last, one morning when I was all alone, I did the next best thing. I left the swing, looked right, looked left, then climbed one of the park trees, just meaning to spy over the wall to see what there was to see.

A ginger cat sat like a sentry on top of the wall—one of those gentle cats that imagine people will always be kind to them. He purred as I edged toward him, so I stopped and tickled him under the chin and he put his head back a little and purred even more loudly.

11

"Miaou," I said, but for his ears alone.

Broken bottles, set along the top of the wall, stood on guard like dangerous glass castles. I stepped carefully in and out of them, and the cat watched me critically. He had no trouble with glass. Every so often I'd catch a glimpse of the house, its weather-beaten tower standing at the end of the main block like an exclamation mark at the end of a magic word. Both word and sign were partly scribbled out by twigs. The window, curving with the curve of the tower, had been painted white for some reason, which made it look as if someone had been using white correcting fluid to change the exclamation into a question mark.

I looked deep into the forest, right, left, then right again, before I leaned forward, grabbing hold of one branch, and stepped gingerly on to the one below it. Both branches bowed under my weight, trying in vain to slide me off. But I was already inside the secret garden.

Garden or forest, it seemed as if I had been working my way toward it from the first time anyone ever told me a story. Invisible paths wound from one tree to another, invisible, that is, until I had scrambled through them once. After that, those paths were as easy to see as the lines on a hand held out, palm upward, toward me.

The times I spent in the forest were short and careful. But as spring moved toward summer I would get up early and spend the first hour of the day among the branches, living what seemed like true life for a while before I came home for real life and breakfast. Mike and Annie thought I went to the playground early because I was too shy to be seen on the swings later in the day. They didn't know that the swings weren't important to me anymore.

True Life

One morning—the one I particularly remember—Miss Credence had finished throwing bread to the birds and had begun to move away when, suddenly, she stopped, studying the ground in front of her as if she had made out an alien footprint. If she had looked up instead of down, she would have seen me quite easily. But by then I almost believed I really was invisible. I felt safe in my high kingdom, and though I *did* step back, I stepped back carelessly.

All I *remember* is taking that step. Then nothing, until I came spinning up out of darkness toward a great flare of sunlight, half eclipsed by a looming black triangle. I blinked and stared again, and slowly a pair of thin hands seemed to condense out of the dark triangle, which darkened still more and became a black cloak. It was Miss Credence herself, squatting in front of me. No wonder I squeezed my eyes shut again.

"You're all right!" she said, a voice from somewhere on a level with my closed eyes. "You're probably bruised, but I'm sure you're all right."

Light was slipping down to me, leaf to leaf, flaring, fading, then flaring again. The newly risen sun had found a gap between the top of the eastern wall and the trees. Miss Credence bent toward me. Between the first and second finger of her right hand

13

was, not a cigar, but a long black cigarette. She would have looked elegant but for her nails, which were bitten so short that the tops of her fingers bulged over them. It made them look like the fingers of a tree-climbing lizard.

"That's better," she said, in a pleasant, dry voice, concerned and yet amused at the same time. "All birds tumble before they fly properly."

I knew I hadn't flown. I had fallen. I was in pain. I tried to move my arm, and opened my mouth, thinking the pain might rush out between my teeth in searing flames. But all that came out was the sound of my own voice, groaning and wordless, in the Credence air.

"I don't think you've broken anything," Miss Credence went on. "Those branches up there broke your fall, and . . . look . . . you got your own back because your fall broke a few branches. Not that it was a true fall, more of a long slide really, with a flight and a flop, right at the end."

I tried to raise myself on my elbows, gasped like some creature trying to breathe for the first time, then slid down again. Looking into Miss Credence's blue eyes, I inched up once more until I was sitting. So far, so bad! I felt sick, *really* sick. Sick in a vomiting way. I began heaving so hard it hurt. Miss Credence pushed my head down between my knees, which is what you are supposed to do with people who are fainting. But I didn't faint, and last night's dinner had gone too far down to be pushed back up again. All I brought up was a lot of spit. The funny thing was that, after this fierce vomiting had worked itself through, I found that just retching and spitting had made me feel better.

"Take it easy," Miss Credence said. "Let the blood flow back into your head."

I leaned against her. She felt like a tree.

"What were you doing up there, that's the question?" she went on. "Adventure, was it? Fun? Well, the adventures we wind up with often aren't the ones we chose in the beginning. If we had the choice, that is."

Old Miss Credence, Mike and Annie had called her. They were interested in her, or in the idea of her at any rate, because she was the great Professor Credence's daughter. Yet, seen close up, she wasn't much older than Annie. She didn't even look old, but she looked—I don't know—eccentric, I suppose. And when we talk about people being eccentric, we often think of them as being old as well. Now, almost nose to nose with her instead of staring down at the top of her hat from among the trees, I was looking into round blue eyes. One of them was set on me, fair and square, the other stared past me, seeming to focus on something that no one else could see.

"You've been doing this for a while, haven't you?" she went on. "Climbing through my trees! I saw you from the tower one morning, scrambling over the wall. And sometimes I've seen your shadow sliding along beside mine. I thought you must be Jorinda, Queen of the Bird People, escaping from someone. Now, tell me you're feeling better."

I was sitting up, feeling my arms and legs (not touching them, just testing them from inside) with some surprise. I had thumped onto a spongy mattress of leaves, layer after layer dropped during a hundred autumns. A meter from where I had landed a rock broke through the soil. I could easily have fallen onto it. A meter was all the difference there was between being alive or, maybe, broken for ever.

"Well?" asked Miss Credence, sitting back on her heels. Then her expression suddenly changed. It became curious . . . intent. "I know you, don't I? You're the girl from the family that bought the house in Edwin Street—the family with the clever mother. You're the deaf child."

She had started off asking, but had ended by telling. I just nodded. Even now, I'm still a cool nodder.

"But you're *not* deaf, are you? Obviously not! Mrs. Lindsay— she's the one who runs that florists on the corner—told me you were deaf, but she's almost always wrong." Miss Credence seemed to be reading answers out of me with no trouble at all. As she spoke, she unfolded, like a stick puppet drawn upward by invisible strings, then held out her arm. I grabbed it. It felt wiry and strong under my fingers.

"Come this way, Jorinda, Queen of the Birds. I'll get you a drink of some kind," she said, and together we sort of bobbed in a strange, crippled dance from under the trees toward the house. The name *Jorinda* rang in my head like a familiar bell, but it wasn't the right time to think about that. For a moment I couldn't help wondering if I had actually died, and was now a ghost. I looked back in case my body was lying, all smashed up, under the tree, but there was nothing there.

In front of the house, to one side of what had once been a lawn, sticking out of long grass, stood a table and three chairs, all covered with a fine green moss.

"Just wait!" Miss Credence said, sitting me down quite graciously in one of the chairs, as if she were offering me a treat. Actually, it hurt to sit, but then everything was hurting. The back of my right hand was scraped gray and blue, and beads of blood stood out across the back of my fingers like jewels set in invisible rings. I didn't wipe the jewels away . . . not immediately. I held my shaking hand out in front of me, and looked at them through half-closed eyes, like a girl admiring an engagement ring.

Over at her door, Miss Credence's long forefinger was pecking at a little panel, a modern blister set under a metal grille, that looked really odd on the old wood and brick. She was tapping in a code. I saw her tap the first key, probably 1, and then tap it again, and I remembered it, because her finger looked just like the beak of a bird, and she had called me Queen of the Birds. After that, she tapped in at least two other numbers and the door clicked very softly, and she pushed it open. By the time she came back with a tray and glasses and a plate I was feeling a lot better, still sore all over, but not dizzy, not sick.

"I've brought you orange juice," she said, "and to tell you the truth I've put a tablespoonful of whisky in it. Not that it's good for girls, or for birds either, but it helps in a crisis. Anyway, my father used to say it did, and he was a clever man."

The fruitcake was rather hard and stale, but the juice was good. I had actually begun to feel wild and adventurous, sitting there, striped with pain (but not unbearable pain), and drinking orange juice with a tablespoonful of whisky in it. This was what successful pirates must feel like, after a battle at sea.

"*Can't* you talk?" Miss Credence asked me. I shook my head, which seemed the simplest thing to do. I was puzzled by her sudden, odd, eager expression, the expression of someone coming upon something that nobody else wants, and seeing a special way of using it.

"Not at all?" she persisted. "Well . . . how sad for you, Jorinda, and for your parents, too. No wonder you want to turn into a bird. I always think flight is a kind of language. Not that I fly myself."

As she spoke she began to fuss over the weedy garden beside the chair, kicking at weeds as if they irritated her.

"Do you ever think of taking on part-time work?" she asked me suddenly.

I was astounded. Out of the blue, Miss Credence seemed to be offering me a job.

"This used to be a beautiful garden, you know," she went on, looking around. "But I find it hard to keep up with it all, and— why pretend? I'm not a gardener. I don't even want to be."

I nodded to show I understood.

"I'm a *private* person," Miss Credence went on. "At least, I enjoy working at my branch, my post office branch that is (the powers-that-be can call it a post shop as much as they like. I'd never work in a shop. Never! An office is entirely different. It's *professional*). Anyhow, once I'm back here and the gate closes behind me I like to be private, and I don't want anyone coming in here for any reason, and then chattering about me out there. So, from that point of view I quite like the idea of a gardener who won't say *anything*."

I really was being offered a job, though jobs of any kind seemed to belong to the outside world, not to the Credence forest.

"What do you think?" she asked me. "Nod or shake! Nine dollars an hour." Nine dollars an hour seemed an incredible amount of money. It was what the people next door to us in Edwin Street paid the woman who came to clean their house twice a week. "Of course, you'd have to earn it. But, in between times, you could go on being Jorinda the Bird Queen up there in the trees."

Besides offering me nine dollars an hour, Miss Credence was inventing a story for me. And I had a vague feeling that I knew the story already. At least the name *Jorinda* seemed familiar, though the idea of the Bird Queen seemed to belong to Credence Country alone.

"So, nod or shake!" she told me.

Nodding felt as if it might be less painful than shaking. I wasn't too sure about being given a name I had not chosen myself, but I loved the idea of that nine dollars an hour.

"It's not that there's anything strange to see around here," Miss Credence went on. "There's nothing that can't be talked about, but I don't *want* it talked about. My life is my own business." And immediately, I knew that her life at the post shop was her real life, but that her life behind the wall was her *true* life. Then I began to wonder if she looked at her two lives with different eyes. That would explain her slightly cross-eyed appearance. Anyhow, I nodded again. "Well, then we can put it on an official footing," Miss Credence said. "I'll ring your mother."

I couldn't . . . well, I didn't . . . explain that Annie was away at a reading conference in Perth, and that she, Miss Credence that is, would have to deal with Mike. Not that it mattered! What Mike decided about our home life was always OK by Annie. A day or two later Mike told me that Miss Credence had contacted him, and offered me a gardening job. Mike had whipped in with a suggestion that Athol was bigger and stronger and could get more done in an hour. Mike and Annie longed for Athol to find work—any work—whereas he seemed to be planning to sit around doing nothing but study for the rest of his life. He was so leisurely about his future, and they were frightened he was turning out to be all cleverness and no character. Anyhow, Miss Credence told Mike that I was the only one she wanted. Apparently she had been quite firm about it.

"What do you think?" Mike asked me. I nodded. "So she's put it to you already?" he asked, looking at me curiously. I nodded again. "Well, it sounds like good luck. Congratulations."

"So! The old Credence place," Athol said that night, looking in at my room. He sounded rather more interested than I had thought he would be. "You'll be going to Squintum's House."

He was making a slightly mean joke about Miss Credence's badly matched eyes, but there was more to the name than that. In a folk story Mike used to read to us from *Old Fairy Tales*, Mr. Fox tells one person after another that he is going to Squintum's House, but you never find out anything about either Squintum or the house. Squintum might have been a man or a woman, the house might have been real or imaginary. In the old fairy story it was a house that everyone seemed to believe in but that was never seen, and you never knew if Mr. Fox really went there or just waited around the corner until people had had enough time to peep into the bag he had left behind him. It was a place with a name, but otherwise quite unknown.

So, after Athol had put the idea of that name into my head, that's what I used to write in the notes I left for Mike and Athol on the blackboard in the kitchen. *Gone to Squintum's House.*

Back soon. Once over the wall I became Jorinda. *Jorinda.* The name still bounced around in my head like a lost echo but never made the connection it was trying to make. I remained the Queen of the Birds, for, as I gardened, Miss Credence would come out, always wearing her black cloak and hat, and make the bird jokes she had begun the moment I tumbled out of the trees at her very feet. And these jokes, which had strangely connected with my own ideas about my life in the trees, turned into an ongoing story about the Bird Queen, Jorinda, and her great enemy, Nocturno the Prince of Darkness. Miss Credence didn't so much *tell* the story as gossip her way through it, snatching fragments out of the air while staring out into the forest, smoking as she spoke. And for a while, just in the beginning, having a name somehow made my secret life seem truer than ever.

Yet before I had fallen out of the trees I had been able to climb and scramble through Squintum's Forest, leaving all names behind me. Being nameless had been a kind of freedom. Now, whenever I was up in the branches I knew I was *allowed* to be there, and that I was casting a shadow in the kingdom below. The name was a leash that could be used to twitch me into place. And now, when I came down from the trees, in a way it was like feeding at Miss Credence's feet, along with all those other birds. I began to miss the way it had been . . . the coming and going, without any name or game.

Then, one morning, soon after this uneasiness had started to make itself felt, the door of our house in Edwin Street opened, and there was Ginevra, back home, and not alone, either. But what happened on that strange, crowded Saturday was all in real life—not in the heart of the forest, but in the heart of the family.

—— Part Two ——

Real Life

Real is what everyone agrees about. True is what you somehow know inside yourself. At any rate that's how I had it worked
out back then. You could go in and out of true life, but it had no
beginning and no end. Real life always began with breakfast.

Our breakfast wasn't a table meal. We all arrived at different
times, chose what we wanted and ate it according to different
rules. Mike, Annie and Sap moved around while they ate, but
Athol and I had definite places, and stuck to them. Nobody ever
took breakfast back to their bedroom, and now I think it must
have been because, as well as eating, we all wanted to listen in
on everyone else's life.

Some of us pretended not to. Athol sat at the table, his head
clasped by his Walkman, and a big book propped in front of him.
He had a notebook and a pen beside him, and every now and
then he'd scribble something down . . . some fact he'd run to a
standstill. I came to imagine the poor fact lying there, panting
and helpless, and Athol ruthlessly fixing it into his notebook,
not so much with the point of his pen as with a skewer of words.
Every book Athol read was about five hundred pages long. I often
checked on things like that when no one was looking.

Voices came in through the open door between the dining
room and the kitchen.

"Don't mash up your cornflakes," Mike was telling Sap, so I
knew she'd reached the stage of smothering cornflakes in sugar
and mashing them into pulp with the back of her spoon. But Sap
was talking at the same time as Mike, half shouting, the way she
often did, and laying down strict rules about her toast. I could

hear her skipping from one foot to the other in time to her own instructions, and probably splashing drops of milk from her bowl of cornflakes onto the kitchen floor.

"I want that *currant* bread," she was saying—(*skip! skip!*)—"and I don't want it dark. I want it just a little bit brown"—(*skip! skip!*)—"and the currants sort of soft . . . sort of *melting* . . . on the top. And butter thick enough for me to *scumble* around the edge."

"Make it yourself," suggested Mike. "Then you'll be sure to get it right." There was a twang from the toaster. "Annie!" he yelled. "Toast!"

"*Scumble!*" Sap repeated loudly, thinking he'd missed her obscure and preposterous word. "It's not good manners to *scumble*, not with food." She waited a second, but Mike didn't ask her what the word meant. "It means rubbing the butter in with my *finger*," she cried at last.

Someone shuffled backward along the veranda that ran past the dining room window. There was a crash as a load of planks was dropped onto other planks. Inside the house, beyond the door to the hall, footsteps came rapidly toward the dining room. Out on the veranda someone began sawing busily. Motley, our tortoiseshell cat, leapt up onto the back of a chair, and Windcheater, the fluffy black cat, sneaked out of the kitchen, flat to the floor, as if he were guilty of some terrible crime.

Every sunny morning, light came in through the window at the side of the dining room and filled the gap between the wall and the side of the blue armchair. I would get my bowl of muesli and a slice of toast, and sink into that secret puddle of gold, with the bottom shelves of the floor-to-ceiling bookcase rising behind me. I wasn't exactly hiding. I just liked that patch of sunshine, and, not solitude exactly, but being on the edge of things with all those stories guarding my back.

Behind me and just over my head were two whole bookshelves filled with copies of the same book. *Average-Wonderful*, said the words on the spine, and then in smaller print, *Annie Rapper*. They were hardcover books, different reprints, or the same title in other languages. Below these were paperbacks, tapes, videos . . . thirty copies of *Average-Wonderful* in different forms. Halfway along the third shelf, red and yellow spines suddenly gave way to shiny blue ones, not quite as cheerful, but thicker and more commanding. *Bright Babies*, said white print down the spine. *Annie Rapper*. This time the author's name was bigger than the title of the book.

These were the shelves you saw as you walked around the room, but below them, hard to see because of the big, blue chair, were other shelves full of books that had belonged to Mike and Annie when they were children, and then to Ginevra and Athol, and then to me and Sap. *The Jungle Book*, *The Secret Garden*, *Old Fairy Tales* and a whole lot of others with faded letters and peeling spines. *Make me true*, they would say to me, over and over again. *Make me true.*

The door to the hall opened.

"Where's Hero?" called Mike from the kitchen as Annie burst through from the hall, smiling and strong.

"Hello, everyone! Love you all," she shouted. "Happy Saturday!" Athol looked over the top of his glasses. I stretched my arm up over the arm of the chair and waved good morning.

Annie didn't go into the kitchen, but reached through the

25

doorway, waggling her fingers, not waving to anyone, just begging Mike to put something delicious in them. Then the door to the veranda opened. Wind rushed in triumphantly. The pages of Athol's book set up a chattering whisper as Colin Brett, one of the builders, a short, sharp-faced, smiling man, edged through, carrying a couple of trestles folded flat. The wind lifted his thin brownish hair, and ran its fingers affectionately over his bald spot. Windcheater shot from beneath the table and in under the dresser, where he crouched, glaring. The presence of strange men and machines in the house was driving him mad. Motley stayed cool. A scornful smile was permanently set in under her whiskers.

"I'd watch those mogs," said Colin to no one in particular. "Cats go missing around here. The Olivers at the top of Credence Crescent have lost two cats in the last six months . . . expensive ones, a Siamese and an Abyssinian. Probably stolen."

"No one would steal ours," cried Sap from the kitchen, scumbling with her toast. "No such luck!"

Mike was sliding toast between Annie's twiddling fingers.

"New nail polish?" he asked. "Vampire blood?"

Annie grinned, and made clawing gestures at the air with her empty hand.

"Looks great to me," said Colin, edging by.

"Thanks, Colin," Annie replied. "Man of taste there!"

Since the builders, Colin and Kevin Brett, had started work on the new upper story, they seemed even more at home in the dining room than we did. They came and went, doing important things that they didn't have to explain . . . well, not totally. "Just checking those old joists," they would say. Things like that. They joked with Mike, though they also looked at him with pity because he was a man doing housework, and passed on clever tips from their wives. They offered Annie stories about the way they brought up their own children.

"Obviously an expert on nails," Annie said.

"Enjoy the compliment!" Mike advised Annie rather sourly as the hall door closed behind Colin and his trestles. "We're paying weekend rates for it."

Annie sat down with her back to the table, holding the toast daintily, bending forward so that buttered crumbs would not fall on her shirt or her cream-colored jeans. She looked both casual and dressed-up. Her long hair, rinsed a reddish brown, sat coiled like a warm serpent on top of her head. But I thought she looked tired. On this particular morning she had a soft, almost pulpy look, as if her flesh wasn't quite sticking to her bones.

"Now, don't hurry!" Mike called, fussing over her from the kitchen. "Chew every mouthful twenty times. You're in plenty of time."

"I am a bit jumpy!" Annie admitted, talking around her toast and sometimes through it. "It isn't going to be one of those easy-going, local conferences where you automatically know miles more than anyone else. Delegates from Australia *and* the USA! I want to look great, but *accidentally* great . . . as if I've just scrambled into whatever happened to be lying around, and it just happens to be terrific. Sling me that tea towel, darling. This toast is just a whisker crumbly. One spot of grease will screw up the whole effect. I'd better drape something around myself."

"Sit at the table," suggested Mike. "It's safer . . . and less trouble, too." But he came out from the kitchen bringing her the tea towel, and actually tied it around her neck so that her blue silk shirt was protected. I saw him touch her cheek as if he, too, thought her flesh might be floating around her skeleton, rather than fastened to it securely.

"How are you feeling?" he asked her in a low, private voice, his lips barely moving.

"Oh, you know!" said Annie. "Hanging in there! Thank God it doesn't last long."

"There's what's-her-name from the USA," shouted Sap, determined to be heard. "Professor Barber." She'd had heard all about this conference before. We all had. "A lot of snollygosters."

"You're up to S, are you?" Mike asked her dryly, taking notice of her words at last. "Only eight letters to go. Thank God!"

"Ha! Ha! Then I'll begin all over again," Sap warned him.

It was Kevin Brett's turn to edge in through the door, angling a couple of long, battered planks whose ends swung across one corner of the table, seeming to miss Athol by inches. Athol swayed back just the right amount, without even glancing up from his book, so I knew he was listening to everything going on around him, though he was pretending not to.

Through the open door came the sound of a busy car rushing by, then stopping in a screeching hurry.

"Watch out!" Kevin called, still angling planks, and Annie leaned back in turn.

"Snollygoster!" shouted Sap. "A snollygoster's a sort of wicked politician," she added, blowing out a few toast crumbs along with the explanation while the wind carried the sound of outside voices inside.

"Someone who does a bit of moral scumbling?" suggested Athol, more to confuse than encourage her. Perhaps he realized that joining in with a comment like this proved he had been listening after all, because he hastily bent to scribble a note in his notebook.

The phone rang. "I'll get it," Annie shouted. "It'll be for me." She leapt up, toast and all, curved herself to let the last section of the planks swing by, then slid into a part of the room where I couldn't see her anymore.

"Annie Rapper," I heard her cry happily. She always announced her name when she answered the phone. Everyone else in the family just gave the phone number, but Annie was always sure she was the one who was wanted, and mostly she was right.

"Carrington!" she cried. "Great! *I* was going to ring *you*." I heard Mike groan a little.

"Carrington!" shouted Sap. "Bloody Carrington! He's got this great sloppy crush on Mum, hasn't he? I reckon he wants to have *sex* with her."

"Shut up! He'll hear you!" hissed Mike. "Don't put ideas into his tiny, academic head. And don't swear!" he added quickly, though you could tell he didn't really mind Sap swearing over Carrington.

"They all do it," said Kevin as he and Colin went back past the kitchen door, making for the veranda again. "I hear my boy sometimes when he doesn't know I'm listening in. Jesus, it raises the hair on the back of my neck, and it *has* to come from school because his mum and I don't swear, well, not in front of kids, anyway."

He shut the door on his last words.

"If I say that consciousness is defined by language, we'll have a whole lot of argument about what consciousness actually is," Annie was telling Carrington. "I think it's defined in the beginning by self-addressed speech, which is something different from inner speech. Inner speech is a form of dreaming." (We often heard that sort of discussion first thing in the morning.) "Never mind! I'll put it on disk, and I'll bring that printout, and . . . what? Oh, the seminar program!"

On the veranda, through the closed door, I heard the Bretts saying, "Morning. Great day!" to someone who was walking up our front steps. "Gawd, what happened to *you?*" Kevin added, sounding as if something had really shocked him.

"It's a *beautiful* day," said a voice, faint but clear on the other side of the door. "It's great to be alive."

I think everyone stopped dead. Even Athol, who was sitting quite still, seemed to grow stiller.

The door opened.

"Hello, everyone! Surprise! Surprise!" cried the voice. "Kill the fatted calf. Show the brute no mercy! I'm *home.*"

I peered round the edge of the chair. Mike stepped into the frame of the kitchen door, his mouth hanging open.

"There are enrollments from Auckland," Annie muttered into the phone, but now there was no interest in her voice. It had all flowed into her face, which was opening out with a sort of shocked happiness.

"Remember *me?*" said Ginevra.

She looked like a smashed-up angel, head bandaged, left arm plastered and suspended in a sling. There she suddenly stood, after four years of vanishment, more battered than when she had left, smiling at us all and delighted by our amazement and horror.

Real Life

"Oh God! What have you *done* to yourself?" cried Annie, still holding the phone to her ear. They were the first words she had actually spoken to Ginevra in all those four years.

"Only a little creative havoc," Ginevra said airily. "Nothing to worry about."

"No, no! Not *you*, Carrington." Annie glared irritably into the phone as if she could actually see a bewildered Carrington at the other end of the line. "Just a family thing! Listen, I'll have to go . . ."

Ginevra half wore a leather jacket, by which I mean it was draped across her left shoulder. The right side of her face was a savage bluish red, and so swollen that the eye was a mere slit between puffy lids. The other side was extremely pale.

"Slight complication in my chosen career," she said, gently rapping the plaster on her left arm with the knuckles of her right hand. One half of her mouth smiled, while the other half lost itself, as it tried to twist over the surface of her swellings.

"Carrington, I'm hanging up, right? Family crisis," Annie was saying impatiently.

Ginevra looked toward the open door.

"Come on in, Sammy," she called. "They won't bite you."

A boy appeared. He was about thirteen or fourteen, older than me anyway, part Maori or part Pacific Islander, or maybe even Spanish. I couldn't tell. Middling dark, anyway, with a proud, handsome look. He was carrying a basketball under one arm, and wore huge, baggy clothes. Big letters marched across the front of his T-shirt. *Boston Celtics*, they said. He wore a baseball cap, jammed on sideways, and curls came out of that little open place above the elastic that usually goes at the back. The sides of his head had been shaved, mind you. It was only the hair on top that had been allowed to grow long.

"This is Sam, my main man," said Ginevra. "When he heard my name was Rapper he knew we were meant for each other."

"Ginny, what *has* happened to you?" asked Mike, holding out his arms, dropping them, then half holding them out again, longing to hug Ginevra, but frightened of the sling and bandages and bruises. "What'll happen if I touch you?"

"Oh, I'm firmly held together by faith and astonishment," said Ginevra, hooking her good arm around his neck. "Great, new house! Benallan! Very up-market."

"You'll love it," said Mike. "There's plenty of room," he lied. "Until you find a place of your own, that is," he added wildly. He was in a bit of a panic.

"A place of my own?" cried Ginevra. "We've only just stepped through the door, and you're trying to move us on?"

"No!" cried Mike. "No, I swear it! I just don't want to sound too straight-off possessive ... you know ... too *fatherly*. Oh damn!" But Ginevra laughed and kissed him. Annie, still trying to shake Carrington off, held out her hand with the red, painted nails, as if she wanted her fingers, at least, to be included in the hug.

"OK! It's a political decision. Let's leave it at that," she exclaimed. "Carrington! Sorry! Must, *must* go!"

"Just hang up on him!" Ginevra suggested, really looking at her for the first time. "Go on! Prove you *really* want to!"

"Ginevra, where the *hell* have you been?" Mike said. Then he turned and looked wildly at the boy called Sammy. "Look, I'm sorry—er—Sammy. You're really more than welcome. Just give us a moment to . . . "

"*Hell* counts as swearing," shouted Sap. "Ginevra, it's me, Sap! Remember me?" She pranced in front of Ginevra, holding out her arms.

"Sap?" said Ginevra. "Sammy, I warned you about my little sister, Sap."

"Yes! Later! Later!" Annie said, freeing herself from Carrington at last.

"Oh, Ginevra!" she cried, even before the receiver had slammed down into its cradle. "Why didn't you let us know . . ."

"Because I didn't know myself!" Ginevra said. "I meant to be really cool—just shoot through. But I've been in two accidents. The best one was a car crash, and the worst one was a man . . . Sammy's father. I mean, we were a bit of an item, him and me, but now he's dumped us. He's taken off, leaving no address. So here we both are. But we won't be any trouble apart from . . . you know . . . just the usual abuse and leaving dirty clothes all over the floor. Hang on a moment. I'll get the rest of my stuff."

"Hey, let me," said Sammy, in a voice that had begun to break.

He and Ginevra vanished onto the veranda, almost colliding in the doorway. The wind roared in again, swooping under the curtains, which billowed out into the room like flowery ghosts. Mike and Annie looked at each other.

"Better or worse?" hissed Annie. Mike pulled a face, shrugged, and mouthed something back at her. "What shall I *do*?" Annie asked in a desperate whisper."Go on! You're good at life. Tell me!" But Ginevra was already coming in from the veranda. A bag overflowing with dirty washing swung from her right hand like dead prey. Sammy followed with a blue hiker's pack hitched over one shoulder. Even before the door closed behind her, Ginevra began talking.

"So, Sammy, you've met Sap and my father, Mike, and you've half met my mother, Annie. Now, that one sitting at the table, being ever so laid back, is Athol. Say hello, Athol! I know you're bursting with curiosity."

"Of course I am!" Athol said, pushing his headphones back so that they hung around his neck. "I was just catching my breath again. Love the new look, kid. It makes us all feel guilty, no trouble at all." And he came round from behind the table to hug her delicately, as if she were cut out of tissue paper. Over his shoulder, Ginevra suddenly caught sight of me . . . or a bit of me, anyway . . . enough to recognize. "Ah ha! Sam, see that eye peering out from behind the blue chair. That's the eye of Hero, the world's quietest Rapper. Hero, just shout hello to Sammy."

"*She* won't shout anything," cried Sap, glad to give Ginevra some alarming news. "She never says a single, solitary word. Not one."

Ginevra looked from me to Mike to Annie, then back to me again.

"She's turned into an elective mute," Sap went on, sounding as if she were quoting from *Mrs. Byrne's Dictionary of Unusual, Obscure and Preposterous Words* once more. "That means she could talk if she wants to, but she never does."

"Doesn't *that* upstage you?" Athol asked Ginevra. "What's a broken arm compared with three years of silence?" He smiled his sly smile. "The arm *is* broken, is it?"

"Oh, yes, in two places," Ginevra replied, sounding absent-minded, as if a broken arm didn't really bother her. "Doesn't Hero ever talk? Not ever?"

"Only to Athol," said Annie, and at last Ginevra turned and looked straight at her.

"Look, Annie—about you and me—" she began. "Don't let's try to say anything *meaningful*. Let's just run on. Hang loose! At least for a bit."

We all watched Ginevra and Annie hug one another, just as people, clustered in front of a television set, watch the end of a miniseries. But this wasn't an end. It was the beginning of a new episode.

The door opened and Colin Brett came through again.

"We'll just get that last bit of scaffolding in place," he said to Mike. "And then we'll be all set for Monday morning. We might need to turn the power off, but we'll let you know, so that you can get yourself organized." He had already told us this. Really, he was just nosing in to find out what was going on.

"I have to go," Annie declared. "You're right, Ginny. No rushing into things." She ran to the hall door, stopped, looked back, opened her mouth, pulled a face, shut her mouth again, and vanished into the hall.

"Wow!" said Sap. "I thought she'd say a million times as much as that."

Sammy began to bounce his basketball. It made a surprisingly loud, thudding noise, and he looked around guiltily before catching it and tucking it back under his arm again.

"Have you had breakfast?" Mike asked him. I could see he was dithering. He wanted to concentrate on Ginevra, not her hanger-on. However, he was doing his best. "Can I get you something? Muesli? Toast? Tea?"

"We're into sausages and eggs," Ginevra declared, answering for Sammy. "To hell with those healthy breakfasts!"

"You certainly don't look as if you've made a priority of health," Athol remarked. "How did you get here?"

"Danny—that's Danny Stahlman, my boss—brought us," Ginevra said. "I did ask him in, but he had to push on to Dunedin. Actually, he was happy to get shot of us. I'm no sort of asset in this state."

"Your boss?" said Mike doubtfully, as if any boss of Ginevra's was a fabulous animal he could hardly believe in. "Is he Sammy's father?"

"No way!" said Ginevra. "Sammy's father is the best-looking brute in the world."

"Well, tell us everything," Mike suggested. "What have you been doing for the last four years?"

"It's a long story," Ginevra said. "I'll tell you later."

Annie swept back into the room, carrying a narrow black dispatch case with gold on the corners, and her laptop slung over one shoulder. She was wearing a blue jacket with gold buttons and she had put on lipstick. In spite of her designer jeans, there was nothing accidental about her polish and power. She had taken her face in hand and had somehow slapped it firmly back onto its bones for the day.

"Wow! Far out!" exclaimed Ginevra, stepping back, shading her eyes with her good hand, as if Annie were giving off heat. But Annie had something she just *had* to say.

"Ginny," she cried, speaking quickly, so she could get it out before Ginny cut her off with some smart-arse line. "I'm just so . . . *happy* to see you home . . . just thrilled . . . " Her voice quavered into nothing.

"Oh, damn!" Ginevra cried impatiently, turning her back on Annie. "Don't start! Can't you see I'm much too frail to put up with niceness?"

"I'm so glad to see you . . . " Annie began again, but once more she couldn't finish.

"I know! I know!" said Ginevra. "Mum, don't! I know all that, or I wouldn't be here. Don't cry all over that great makeup job."

Annie hugged Mike. She did this every morning, but on this particular morning there was something different and desperate about the hug. "Sorry to leave you with all this."

"Go on! Get out!" said Mike, smiling. "I can run this lot with one hand tied behind my back."

He wouldn't let her tear herself away immediately, but held her, brushing a bit of cat hair off her shoulder. Then he kissed first one of her eyelids and then the other.

"Oh, yuck!" muttered Sap, who talked a lot about sex but hated any sign of it in parents. Mike took no notice.

"Don't forget!" he said to Annie, without saying what it was she had to remember.

"You're a saint." Annie suddenly sounded completely in charge of herself again. "See you later. I'll stop off at the supermarket on the way home. I've got the list, but I'll sling in some extra stuff and a few treats. Ring the office if you think of anything else we need. Tina will be there as weekend backup, doing photocopying and setting up the slides. She'll take messages. Oh, and I'm taking the Peugeot."

"Of course," said Mike, sounding resigned.

The door closed behind her.

Ginevra somehow managed, sling and all, to leap in a lopsided, limping way across the room, wincing as she did so, and to pull the door open after Annie.

"Hey, Annie," she shouted. "I've just thought of something! Do you think we *invent* mathematical ideas or do we *discover* them? I mean, do we make them up and put them into nature, or are they in nature already, waiting to be found?"

"Oh, ha! Ha!" Annie called back. She had heard it all before. We all had. In fact, we had it on video.

But when I heard those words I felt the world crush in on me. Suddenly, there was too much going on—the ghosts of too many old arguments in the air. And then yet another voice blew in from outside. Rappie! Rappie, the born-again jogger, looking in for a Benallan breakfast, and probably winding herself up to criticize Annie, not with words, but sideways looks and significant nods, for taking off on a Saturday morning, leaving Mike with all the housework. I leapt up as if I were looking forward to seeing Rappie, but I was really planning to take off for Squintum's House until most of the fuss was over.

"Hero!" cried Ginevra, hooking me with her good arm. "You can't just walk by the prodigal child like that."

"No use talking to *her*," said Sap.

"She can *hear*, can't she?" Ginevra called over my shoulder as we hugged each other. "And I can talk enough for both of us."

But by then Rappie was through the door, shouting, "Another seminar, I suppose!" And *then* she saw Ginevra, and cried out, her voice changing, her sharpness melting, because Ginevra had always been her first, darling grandchild. And what with the exclaiming, and Sap shouting, and one thing and another, nobody really noticed me drifting out into my own Saturday.

"What sort of a welcome is this for you?" I heard Rappie crying. She could hardly believe that Annie had driven off as if Ginevra's sudden appearance was nothing out of the ordinary.

"Don't fuss! Don't fuss!" Within a mere two seconds, Ginevra was sounding slightly impatient. As I reached the door, I had to push past Sammy, flattened against the wall, quite overlooked by all us Rappers. Sammy and I looked into one another's eyes as I went by, and then we both looked away. The door wasn't quite shut, and I slipped through it, with Windcheater dashing past my ankles, anxious to lose himself in the bushes in the garden.

I certainly took Colin and Kevin Brett by surprise. There they stood on our veranda, one holding a level, the other a saw, listening intently to the words of a private family soap opera that were squeezing out from under the door.

"Hi," said Colin, smiling more or less in my direction, and immediately laying the level along a bit of wood, pretending that that's what he had really been doing all along.

I slid by, down the path and through the gate.

"I don't know," I could hear Kevin saying. "They might have made a lot of money out of telling other people how to bring up kids, but I reckon I could give them a few pointers."

I turned east, and walked toward the forest and my true life. What with it being Saturday, what with Ginevra turning up like that, I was going to Squintum's House much later in the morning than I usually did. But, as I walked, I gathered the nor'west wind around me like a sort of cloak, and felt myself swelling to my true size.

True Life

In spite of rattling pages and billowing curtains, I had not realized how strong that wind was. But as I ran down Edwin Street it seemed to snatch my steps from under my feet before they had been properly finished so that I felt as if I were about to fly.

And then the wind swept the sound of children's voices to me, almost as if it knew I would never go into the playground, climb the trees, and run along the wall, in and out of the broken glass, if there were anyone there to watch me. Instead, I ran on past the Park Place turnoff, deeper into Credence Crescent.

Garage doors and gardens curved ahead. I leapt along, past low fences and open gateways. And then the Credence wall began . . . old mossy bricks, crumbling mortar, and blades of grass growing from all sorts of little gaps. I ran on past KILL THE PUNKS, an old inscription, red letters already a little mossy, reached NO NUKES, and then THE ONLY TRUE CONFORMITY IS IN THE GRAVEYARD, and passed them by. *Ginevra home!* said a voice in my head, not my own voice, the voice of some storyteller who always traveled with me.

These days I had two ways of getting into the Credence forest, the high road (over the wall), and the low road, which meant going in by the front gate. I had been given the code, you see. But, as I leapt and sprang purposefully toward the gate, family thoughts loped along like a pack of wolves, easily keeping up with me.

Ginevra! Ginevra home again! said a storytelling voice inside my head. I could almost see the words floating past my eyes in *Old Fairy Tales* print.

Where the crescent reached the top of its curve and began to fall back toward Benallan Drive stood two tall gates, all spikes and spirals, held together by a rusting chain, and a padlock so choked with dirt and rust that nobody could have fitted a key into it anymore. Not that it mattered. These gates had never once been opened since we had come to live in Benallan. They hadn't been opened for years. But to the left of the big gates, a second, smaller gate, taller than I was but not very much wider, filled a narrow slot in the wall, and a gray metal box was set into the stone beside it. This box had a lid which lifted to reveal a series of little keys with numbers on them.

The street, curving away from me on either side, was still perfectly empty, but I hunched myself around the box, hiding it from . . . I-don't-know-what . . . hiding it from the wind, I suppose, as I tapped in the code, 0-8-0-9, and listened for the soft click as the lock on the smaller gate disengaged. As I pushed, it opened noiselessly, then swung shut behind me and clicked, locking itself once more.

The wind shook itself through leaves and bushes, and I began to hear birds . . . no single song but a mix of twitterings . . . as I walked into the restless shadow under a double line of old linden trees, and up the wide, neglected drive set with oval puddles, and flanked by yarrow, flowering docks and nightshade. Beyond the lindens were oaks and a few gum trees, Australian wattles, then a line of huge camellias growing against the stone wall on the eastern side of Squintum's forest. Long, thin, strangling grasses and frail seedling sycamores stretched up from the forest floor, but you could tell they'd never make it. Somewhere behind me I heard the sigh of the city; somewhere in front of me I heard a door slammed sharply. The sound had an edge that seemed to cut into me. But I didn't hesitate. I walked on through the forest.

And now I found that, on this particular day, real life was refusing to step back as it usually did. Family voices ran through my head. *Ginevra home again!* said a triumphant voice, but this time the voice wasn't a storytelling one. It was Ginevra's own.

If you write a book telling other people how to bring up children, your own family life must prove that your ideas actually work. Annie's first book, *Average-Wonderful*, did really well. The publisher sold editions in Australia, in the United Kingdom and even in the United States. "We really hit the big time," Annie used to say. "There's a huge market out there." She always laughed at her own success, as if it did not really matter. Nevertheless she lived turning toward it like a sunflower following the sun.

Her book suggested that every child in the world was a sort of genius at the same time as being perfectly ordinary, and that, if children were properly treated, the genius would naturally flower. No big deal: it just would! If children were *lured up* (Annie's words) they would all blossom into wonderful people. There are about a million books that say the same thing, but Annie's particular book really caught on. I think it was partly because Annie herself believed in it so much, and *looked* so great talking about it. But it wasn't just that. In the beginning she seemed to have proof that her ideas would work. The proof was Ginevra.

"You can't think about nothing," Ginevra says in one television interview (because she was interviewed a thousand times, mostly in teachers' colleges and education departments and so on). "Just thinking about 'nothing' turns 'nothing' into 'something.' "

She says this, then she pauses and smiles. The interviewer smiles too, encouraging her to go on. "Once you make up a *name* for 'nothing' you make it a little bit real," Ginevra adds. She was about ten, I think.

"What do you say to that, Athol?" asks the interviewer in a soft voice, trying not to frighten a shy animal. But Athol was never shy. He just looks sideways at Ginevra, grinning.

"What about space?" he asks. Back then, he lisped, even though he was eight or nine years old. "Space has a name, but it's a name for *nothing*." They really could talk like that. They still do, given half a chance, though, nowadays, Athol says space is alive with *something*. . . . with virtual particles, whatever they are . . . with *possibility*.

Their pictures, prints of old newspaper photographs, are pinned on the wall behind this new computer, Athol staring straight out into the world, using his long smile to hold it all at bay, Ginevra turning away, and then looking back over her shoulder, inviting someone to follow her.

But I would never follow the trail Ginevra left behind her. I wanted paths of my own, and I suppose that was one of the reasons I visited Squintum's House.

It seemed to drift toward me from behind the trees, and at last I saw it all, even the tower with its whited-out upper window.

I didn't go straight to the house, but headed for the garden shed where I found two garden forks—a big one and a little one. *Ginevra home again!* said that voice in my head. I walked around the curve of the lawn that had become a meadow.

Miss Credence was dancing, turning round and round on a patch of gravel path I had weeded the week before, and whistling softly to herself. I watched her from the other side of the curve of long grass. Beyond her, sitting beside the door, was a black box that reminded me of a camera. As she turned she saw me, smiled, and danced a few swirling steps in my direction.

"Just a little private light-heartedness," she cried self-consciously, but eagerly too, as if she had been longing for me to turn up. "I've been waiting for you. You're late this morning. Where were we up to?"

She was referring to her story . . . the one that had sucked me in. I would bend over a border, struggling with docks and chickweed while Miss Credence leaned against a tree or a wall, talking and gesturing, so that the long black cigarette looked like a short wand, or a pencil writing on the air in letters of smoke. The story was almost about me . . . well, it was about Jorinda (the name that came and went in my memory like light on a cloudy day). Miss Credence's Jorinda was a bird-girl, swooping around the trees of an old forest, pursued by Nocturno, the evil bird catcher. And at times, just as Jorinda seemed to have a lot in common with me, the villain seemed to have a lot in common with Miss Credence. Her voice became more thrilling whenever he came into the story, and she gave him the most interesting things to say. Not only that, the name Nocturno suggested night, and there she was, standing over me, dressed in her black cloak and hat.

At this time of year the ground was hard beneath a light, grayish crust that crumbled to dust when I hit it with the back of the fork. I had sometimes helped Mike in the garden, so I had a rough idea about pulling out weeds and loosening the soil around the plants that seemed as if they ought to be there. I worked among lavender bushes planted against the wall of the house, piling nightshade and docks on a square of green plastic. Often the prongs of the fork jarred and bounced back from soil as hard-packed as bricks, but I struck again and again, turning it a little, pulling out the white, jointed worms of twitch, and rolling back green mats of clover. The heads of lavender, on a level with mine, were white and pink as well as blue. Miss Credence had stopped dancing and now walked up and down on the edge of the long grass, telling her story.

Suddenly, something moved between my hands . . . my own

shadow. It wasn't that the sun had just risen, but it had appeared over a wide bank of cloud that lay along the tops of the hills. The forest behind me was thrust through with wide blades of gold. Miss Credence stopped her storytelling.

"Things are looking a lot better, aren't they?" she called. "You *have* made a difference!"

I suppose I'd made *some* difference, but if she wanted real improvement she needed a whole tribe of gardeners, huge mowers and chainsaws, perhaps even earth-moving machinery. All I'd done was weeding and a little trimming, cutting the wilderness back with the flat of the spade, and giving room to the wide border of perennials that fringed the base of the house.

"Be careful there, won't you? That clover has grown right through the campanula, and it's hard to tell one from the other, the stems are so similar," she said. "Where was I? Oh yes! Jorinda was swooping down on Nocturno. Doing this, the sun came out behind her. What a trick! As Nocturno spun round after her, its first rays fell directly upon him. Remember I told you sunlight was death to him? Immediately, his mask began to melt. Jorinda gasped. There behind the mask she saw . . . " Miss Credence broke off. "What's that on the other side of the campanula? Oh, it's *gypsophila. . . . gypsophila paniculata. . . .* it looks so . . . so *light* in floral arrangements, not that I've ever been interested in flower arranging, but my mother used to love it. Well, she must have. She did a lot of it. Mind you, my father encouraged her. He liked fresh flowers in the house."

Miss Credence had done something she did from time to time. She had brought her story to a certain point and then had somehow sprung back from it as if something in it had *burned* her.

"Now, we used to have a great border of *primula vulgaris*," she said, "the common primrose, that is, but I've rather let them go, and do you know, you can't buy them in any nursery these days. I mean, they have *modern* primroses of all colors at Shelley's Garden Shop, but I don't think of those modern *colored* primroses as real primroses . . . " And then, having pretended enough interest in the garden, she went on, but less cautiously this time.

"Imagine! The black cloak and hat lay there quite empty. Nocturno's dark wisdom had melted in the light, and of course he had to melt with it. There wasn't much else to him beside wisdom. Have you ever seen *The Wizard of Oz*?"

Everyone I know has seen *The Wizard of Oz*. I knew Miss Credence was thinking of the scene where Dorothy throws water on the witch and she shrinks to nothing, shouting that Dorothy has melted all her lovely wickedness. I suppose there was nothing to the witch except wickedness. And the same thing happens in those *Star Wars* films. Obi Wan Kenobi and Yoda both melt away into another state, leaving their empty clothes behind them.

"I picked them up and put them on," said Miss Credence, in a sudden sharp voice. "I mean Jorinda did. The black cloak fitted her exactly."

I looked up from the garden and stared over at Miss Credence, astonished by this turn of events, and by the change in her voice. Noticing my surprise, Miss Credence paused. She was teetering on the edge of her lawn. "I'll get someone in to run a motor mower over this," she said, waving her hand vaguely. "After that you'll be able to maintain it with a hand mower." She had been promising to have this done since I began working for her.

Right now, the lawn was a mass of grass heads. A delicate gold-green surface shimmered in and out of existence above the real surface, almost as if atoms and electrons had had their dance made visible. Through the shimmer I could see green blades thrusting upward, and wild flowers too, tiny pink starry ones, and every now and then a blue one, a single flower on a stem as fine and tough as a green wire.

"There's something I want you to do for me," said Miss Credence. "I want you to take my photograph. Do you know how to work one of these?" The black box by the door really was a camera, as I had guessed. She was opening the little shutter over the lens. "It's got a film in it, and they say that all you have to do is look into the viewfinder, line up the picture and press the button. It focuses itself and adjusts to the light. Isn't that wonderful? I can remember when taking a photograph took ages. I used to hate being photographed when I was a child." I took the camera from her. "Stand over there," she said, "then I won't be looking straight into the sun."

I walked over to the door, which was where she had pointed I should stand, and when I turned, the whole world had changed in half a second.

Miss Credence was suddenly holding a gun under her left arm, and I caught her in the act of lifting a victim from the long grass of the ruined lawn, which had hidden it until then. It was my old friend the ginger cat. She held him by the tail and his head bobbed a little. He had not been dead long. He was still limp. His mouth was open. His tongue stuck out. It was a horror moment, real and true, and I actually felt the world darken around me. My own mouth fell open. I made a sound, which I almost never did, and something inside me began to tremble violently.

Miss Credence was startled, even shocked, by my sound, and when she saw my expression her own face changed. She looked down at the dead cat as if she were slightly perplexed to find herself holding him.

"Oh, yes . . . well . . . " she said. "They prey on birds, and I just can't have that. This whole country was a country of birds once, did you know that? Nothing on four legs. Nothing without wings. Then people brought cats, and cats are not just murderers, they're torturers, too. My father kept this garden strictly free of cats, and I maintain his standards. And, besides, he was a sportsman. People forget that he loved sports. Now, take the photograph."

I must have collected myself in some way as she said all this because I took charge of that deep trembling. After all the country was filled with people who naturally shot animals that had pushed themselves in where they weren't supposed to be. Farmers shot visiting dogs; conservation department men were paid to shoot rats and possums and lots of cats too. I'd even seen photographs of them with their trophies. And, just for a moment there, it seemed as if taking Miss Credence's photograph would be—almost safer. It might have been because Nocturno's own voice, an *iron* voice, had spoken out through her, but it also felt as if I must keep everything smooth, and then I would be able to hide behind that smoothness. I took a first photograph, and then another, remembering the clap of sound with the keen edge, which I had taken to be the noise of a slamming door. All the time I knew there was something mad about what she was asking me to do, but moving smoothly from one thing to another made it seem as if I were *inside* a story, making it happen and not just reading it from a page.

As I took a third photograph, a gust of wind suddenly struck us and brought me what seemed like the scream of the ginger cat's ghost. The sound wasn't loud. It was part of the actual wind, pressed against my ear, then pulled away again. Had I really heard it? I *knew* I had and then, a second later, I just *thought* I had.

But Miss Credence had heard the scream as well. She wheeled around, staring up into the strip of sky between the walls of the house and the edge of her forest, looking as if God had mewed at her, spreading his claws and lashing his tail, from the sky above the tower.

"Did you *hear* anything?" she asked.

I didn't know what to say, and I wouldn't have said it, anyway. I shrugged my shoulders.

"I must have imagined it," said Miss Credence. "Now, while I think about it, there's your pay." Plunging her hand into her pocket, she brought out an envelope with my name written on it in a firm, round hand.

She wasn't just paying me. I realized she suddenly wanted her garden to herself. So I took the envelope, nodded and smiled, and, since I wouldn't go by the trees, not when she was watching me, I set off between the lindens. Puddles, as I jogged toward them, looked like scattered silver coins, but when I reached them and looked down they were nothing but muddy water, after all. I jumped across the fallen branches, the wind chasing behind me now, like a dog seeing me off the property, and as I ran I heard the city begin to mutter in the distance, like an excluded magician. I was glad to hear the city, and more than glad to go. I was frightened of Miss Credence, and frightened by what I had just done—taking that photograph of her holding a dead cat, I mean. I had peered into the viewfinder as obediently and intently as if she had crossed my palm with silver and I were reading a fortune. There had been something about her pose, something swaggering and triumphant, that suggested she had *practiced* it many times before.

Real Life

Miss Credence was right in what she had said. New Zealand had once been a country filled with birds. They had even lived on the ground because they were safe there. There were no enemies to kill them, back then. In the early morning the whole land had rung with song after song.

But people came, and rats came with people, and both people and rats ate birds to stay alive. And then yet *more* people came, and different rats, and then cats to catch rats which caught birds instead. It is strange to think that Ratty in *The Wind in the Willows* was really as bloodthirsty as any stoat or weasel. In any case, people brought the stoats and weasels, too.

I jogged on, and as I came closer to home my family grew stronger and brighter in my mind, and Miss Credence faded a little. The figure in black with the dead cat dangling from her hand seemed more like an illustration than a real person. I was glad to have her fade like that, and happy to find myself thinking instead about Mike and Annie.

Real Life

Mike and Annie had met at Teachers' College in Auckland.

"Your father didn't stand a chance," Annie said, telling Sap and me our family history. "I clapped eyes on him and, *whooomph!*"

"She put out a tongue that was long and red, and swallowed me down like a crumb of bread," Mike would say, smiling at Annie. "It was wonderful." Then they would both laugh.

So they married, and started their married life teaching together at an East Coast country school inland from Gisbourne. When Ginevra was born ("Did you *have* to get married?" Sap asked. "That's our business, not yours," said Mike, smiling mysteriously), Annie gave up teaching the senior class and concentrated on being the most wonderful mother in the world. "I talked to Ginevra even before she was born," Annie would say, telling the story. ("Big deal!" Ginevra would mutter. "She likes the sound of her own voice anyway.")

But Annie's talking was never just sound. She made up mysteries, games, jokes and revelations, told Ginevra stories, asked riddles and sang songs for her. When she took her out at night, they didn't just look at the stars but stared into the spaces between them, as well.

"We only did what most parents do," Annie would explain. "We put our baby at the center of things. Simple!"

But she says it a little more smugly than she realizes. And, anyhow, Athol says no light comes back from the edges of the universe, so, if you can't be sure about the edge you can't be sure about the center, either. I mean the center turns out to be everywhere. You are the center yourself. And what about people like me and Athol who like edges best?

Annie loved being the center. She loved the world. What she shared with Ginevra was not just knowledge but happiness. As she cuddled her little daughter, she looked into her eyes and told her how marvelous being alive was, how marvelous *she* was, just being herself. She did this for all of us, including me, only not as often as she had done for Ginevra because she had grown so much busier by the time I was born, and her time had to be shared.

I think a bit of all this crept back to me as I made my way home to Edwin Street that Saturday. The wind had calmed down, and the Brett brothers had gone home to their own weekend lives. The last of the scaffolding was finally bolted into place, and our whole house was embraced by a frame of steel pipes and planks. On Monday the Bretts would begin peeling off the roof. Fine weather would be highly important to the Rapper family over the next week or so.

As I walked by, the Maxwells, who lived next door, looked over their fence.

"And you can tell your father I'm not happy about *that*," said Mr. Maxwell, pointing at the scaffolding and speaking as if we had already been having a conversation. "You lot will be able to look right down into our backyard."

"Save your breath," said his wife. "That's the deaf one."

"Aren't they all perfect?" said Mr. Maxwell sarcastically. "Hasn't their mum made a fortune from telling other people how to have super kids?"

That's what a lot of people thought, but Annie's first book had been called *Average-Wonderful* with *Average* coming first. And she hadn't pushed Ginevra in front of her to advertise her theories either, though later on, people sometimes said that that's what she had done.

Ginevra's fame began with an accident. Some member of parliament had complained about falling standards of mathematics and science in New Zealand schools (you know the way they always do—everything was always so great in the past before whatever government we have was voted in and spoiled everything). Anyhow, the local television people had decided to make a short item for the evening news. One morning they rolled into Ginevra's classroom with their camera and cables, and Ginevra's teacher picked her out of the class to answer questions.

"I know I used to find math hard and boring," the interviewer began, in the sort of voice interviewers use when they are trying to make out they secretly understand just what it is like to be a kid. "What's it *like*, learning math these days, Ginevra?"

Ginevra's face seemed to open up with happiness at being given the chance to talk on television.

"Well, sometimes I worry about whether mathematics is something we've just made up, or if it was already *in* the world even before we began working it out," she said. Mind you, she was only repeating something she had heard, but she *remembered* it. She had liked the *sound* of the idea. And it must have been amazing to hear words like that flowing from the mouth of a little girl.

Ginevra became a star at the best possible time for Annie's book, *Average-Wonderful: Helping Your Child to Dance with the World*, which appeared in the bookshops a few weeks later, accompanied by blown-up black-and-white shots of Ginevra taken from that exact news item.

"Oh, God!" said Ginevra, ages later . . . years later . . . when someone asked her if the book had influenced her in any way. "We're Siamese twins, that book and me, joined at the navel. We were launched together."

Launching Ginevra and Athol took up a lot of time. Annie and Mike launched them and kept them launched. Annie wrote and lectured, and traveled—sometimes with her entire family—from conference to conference. It was no wonder that they waited a long time before having another baby. There is about a year and half between Ginevra and Athol, but it was eleven years before I was born.

I've worked out that something began to go wrong for Ginevra when I was about four years old, but I don't quite know what it was. By the time I was old enough to follow family arguments Ginevra seemed to feel angry about absolutely everything. "I wish I'd never been born," she used to cry. "Why did you *have* me? Why didn't I have *choice?*" Yet even when she was arguing, anyone could tell Ginevra loved being alive. It was as if she could never be as *much* alive as she wanted to be.

As I reached the veranda I could see Sammy standing on the

top step. He gave me half a smile, but I couldn't work out what sort of smile it was. "Sorry!" it seemed to be saying, then, "Get lost!"—apologizing and attacking at the same time. And then he did something remarkable. He began to chant in a soft, rapid voice, bouncing the ball, clapping his hands, then bouncing it again. The claps and bounces, mixing in with his words, made a brisk rhythm.

"Ever'body's arguing. They're all in there abusing!
So watcha bringing home to us?
And where've you been cruising?"

He stopped. We stared at each other. And then he went on with his chanting and bouncing and clapping, but doing a sort of snaky dance as well, backward and forward along the top step. He made the dancing and bouncing look as easy as talking.

"The dance it keeps on dancing, and the beat it keeps on beating,
And I ain't the sort of chicken who is rapping and retreating.
And I'm not afraid of any dude who's top of the school,
And I'm no sort of airhead, I'm no sort of fool!"

He began jumping lightly from the top step to the one below, then jumping back again, bouncing and clapping all the time.

"Operator! Operator! Get me a line
And I'll dance you out a prophecy that's totally mine.
Zip. Zap. The ball goes slap.

I am bouncing and announcing from all over the map.
Don't mess with me, man. I'm totally clued!
I'm a devil, I'm a dancer, I'm a real cool dude."

Put down like this it doesn't make that much sense, but, as he chanted and danced and bounced, it seemed like a sort of spell— an incantation!

Then his invention ran out, but he still danced and bounced with his mouth partly open, because he was enjoying my surprise. No new words came to him, and yet you could feel the beat of words running through him like electricity as he showed off to me.

Then another voice spoke, a familiar one.

"Hey, Hero!" As I looked around, really startled, it hissed, "Shhhh!"

I couldn't see anyone. "Up here!" the voice said in a stage whisper. It was Sap, crouching in the new scaffolding. A short ladder, battered but serviceable, led from the veranda up to the walkway that now ran right around our house. I could see Sap had found her own city-street version of my forest. But why was she whispering?

"Where did you go to?" she asked, very quietly. "Squintum's House?"

I nodded.

"It's been so exciting here all of a sudden." She looked at Sammy. "Skookum! Skookum!" she said, using one of Mrs. Byrne's preposterous words. Sammy didn't ask what she meant, and nor did I, though she'd used it several times in the last day or two, so I knew it was a way of telling me in private language that she thought he was terrific. I could tell she was planning to fall in love with him. But Sammy didn't look back at her.

"Oh, well! Come on *now!*" Sap hissed, jerking her thumb back toward the point where the walkway reached the eastern corner of the house and, turning at right angles, vanished from sight. "They're all in the sitting room, talking, and Mike sent me down to the shop to buy extra stuff, just to get me out of the way. But if we climb along here we can listen in." So I climbed up the ladder into the scaffolding. "Come on, Sam!" said Sap in a wheedling voice, speaking as if they were already old friends, but Sammy just shrugged and turned away. Sap stopped at the first corner of the house and began whispering at me again.

"Sammy says his father has just dumped him . . . and Ginevra, too. He buggered off while Ginevra was in hospital, and left Danny Stahlman, the boss of the Stock Car Circus, to look after them." Sap enjoys a bit of swearing, but this time I could tell she was quoting what Sammy had said. "That dance he was doing, that's hip-hop. It's a sort of rap, only he says it's *softer* than rap; he says it hasn't got the *hard edge*. And he makes that stuff up, just like *that*. Awesome."

Sap tried to snap her fingers, but only made a slippery sound with them. Then she turned and crawled carefully on, and I followed her denim-covered bottom around the corner.

At last she stopped, so I had to stop as well. We were right above the sitting room window, the same one that the sun shone though every morning, and there we knelt, looking like two wise monkeys. Not that we could see any evil, and we weren't going to speak any—well, I certainly wasn't going to—but I suppose we were both hoping to *hear* a bit. The window below me

58

swam with a distorted reflection of the Maxwells' fence, dark but transparent, so I could peer, at a sharp angle, past the edge of the walkway and right down through the reflection to make out a long slot of chair with a bit of the bookshelf behind it and even a few copies of *Average-Wonderful*.

Along the top of the big window, a little below the walkway we were kneeling on, ran a series of small oblong windows, hinged along the top and filled with that old-fashioned bobbly glass you can't see through. They were all open, and the sound of voices drifted up through them.

"And that's what you've been doing for the last four years?" Mike's voice! He sounded as if he had just been told something he couldn't believe. "Crashing cars?"

"Yes, but crashing them *creatively!*" said Ginevra. "I was the girl star of Danny Stahlman's Stock Car Circus. Haven't you seen us advertised on TV?"

"We still don't watch TV," said Athol's voice. "Annie's terrified that Sap will become addicted to *Pharazyn Towers*. She would, too. We all would."

"You've lost me," Ginevra said. "Oh, hang on! I know! That soap opera on afternoon telly. Well, chalk it up. I'm on Annie's side for once."

"Oh, I don't know," Athol replied. "I mean, everyone says how terrible it is, but I don't think anyone in this family has ever sat through a single episode. So why not? Aren't we average-wonderful Rappers supposed to believe in actually experiencing things rather than blindly accepting authority?"

"It's nothing but a lot of infidelity and incest among two rich families in Auckland," said Ginevra. "And a run-of-the-mill evil businesswoman ruining the chances of her own beautiful sweet-natured daughter. Gross!"

"Crashing cars sounds pretty gross to me," said Mike. I thought I could *hear* him shaking his head at her.

"Don't knock it. It's applied mathematics," said Ginevra. "Take the T-Bone, for example. I plough my car into another car. So far so good!" I heard a slap and imagined her smacking the fist of one hand into the palm of the other, but then I realized she couldn't possibly do that. Perhaps she smacked her own knee. "Now . . . if I hit at the proper angle and the right speed, the car I'm driving flips up on end at right angles to the stationary car. 'T' bone! Get it? Or, if I alter the pace and the approach, the car I'm driving somersaults right over the top of the standing one. I leap out, caper around, bow! When people cheer for me they're really cheering for mathematics."

"I just can't believe I'm hearing this!" cried another voice. Rappie had obviously been unable to tear herself away from the family reunion. "Oh, Ginny, you were such a clever girl! You could have been anything you wanted to be."

"I have been anything I wanted to be," Ginevra answered indignantly. "I wanted to crash cars, and there was such a fuss after I did the first one (not that I did it on purpose) that I had to run away and join the circus. And it's not just easy, you know. It's every bit as hard as being an accountant or an engineer. Harder!"

"Oh, I know, dear, but . . . crashing old cars. It seems so violent."

"I *am* violent," exclaimed Ginevra.

"How long have you been back in New Zealand?" Athol's

voice drifted from the far side of the room. "I mean we all thought that you were somewhere in the depths of Western Australia, but you seem to have been back here long enough to get the drift of *Pharazyn Towers*. It's not showing over in Oz, is it?"

"I've been back three weeks. Almost three weeks. Mostly in the north," said Ginevra. There was silence, and when she spoke again, she sounded as if she were defending herself. "Well, let's face it, you all get along better without me. And what am I missing? I walked in this morning, and nothing had changed . . . not one thing! Annie was yakking in conference jargon. Mike was getting breakfast like a New Age male saint, and Athol was still hunched over a great fat book taking his little notes. God, Athol, I think it was the exact same book you were reading four years ago. At least I've been moving, I've been *living*, not just sitting around."

"Couldn't you take this accident as a nudge from fate? A sign it *is* time to sit around for a bit?" Mike asked, managing to sound like a good father, worried, but not too critical, not *looming* or anything.

"What? Teach physics at some high school?" exclaimed Ginevra. "No, thanks! When you've lived mathematics the way I have, trusting my whole life to equations, writing them up on a blackboard would be a bit of a comedown."

"Who said anything about teaching?" said Mike. "What about some research job? Something in engineering, say? Or get a qualification. There must be a few jobs left. And you were brilliant, Ginny."

"Not quite as brilliant as David Ching, however," said Ginevra, her voice sharpening.

"Forget David!" exclaimed Mike, sounding rattled for the first time. "Don't tell me you've only come home now to do a bit of triumphant bleeding in front of us."

Ginevra didn't answer him.

"My specialty is a little sequence, *car to topless in ten seconds*," she said, sounding really pleased with herself. "I drive an old car at high speed in under an iron bar that just rips the whole top off it. I have to time it immaculately."

"So what went wrong this time?" asked Athol. "Did you forget to duck?"

"I'd have lost my whole head if I had," said Ginevra. "No! I just misjudged a perfectly ordinary approach to a ramp . . . had a lot on my mind, lost my concentration for a fraction of a second, and wham! Never mind! I needed a break."

"Well, you certainly got what you needed," said Athol. "You won't find me insulting you with sympathy."

"Oh, you're so clever," Ginevra cried. "So, why are you still sitting around at home taking scratchy little notes, and leaving me to have all the adventures?"

(But anyone listening would have been able to tell that Athol and Ginevra were old friends who understood one another well.)

"I'm going to do my master's," Athol said. "New Historicism. Why do some people accept revelation and others reject it?"

"Boring, boring!" Ginevra chanted. "Annie's been there, done that! Trodden everything *flat!* Anyhow, there's just no such thing as correct knowing."

"So, perhaps I'm being lazy as well as clever," said Athol. "And maybe that's clever in itself. We'll see."

"And what's this about Hero not talking?" Ginevra demanded, switching the topic suddenly. "That's not in the family tradition. It must be a bit of a drag for Annie."

"It doesn't seem fair," said Rappie. "Poor Mike has worked so hard with you children . . . well, Annie has too, of course . . . so why have things turned out to be so difficult? I mean, imagine having a child who just doesn't speak."

"Hero's great," said Mike, like a father with good positive attitudes. "She reads. She writes. And *she*, let me point out, has a job. She gets *paid*."

"That certainly puts me in my place," said Athol, not sounding particularly humble while Ginevra cried, "I've been paid, too. Sammy and I are quite well off, actually. I've got thousands of dollars."

"Hero will talk again when the time is right for her," said Mike, but sounding as if he were delivering a little sermon to unbelievers. I had heard him preach this message before, but I am not sure that he believed it himself.

If I ever wanted to, I could put on a video, and see myself, five years old and reading aloud in a soft, shy voice from *A Christmas Carol*, then looking up into the camera and smiling, almost as if I were the sort of star that Ginevra had been. The Teachers' College had been making a short documentary on New Zealand reading schemes for Annie to use when she visited a college of higher education in Melbourne.

"Ginevra, my oldest daughter, is definitely our word child," I heard Annie say to someone behind my back, a moment after I had smiled that smile. "But Hero's the quiet one." I turned, and found my mother looking over at me, as if my quietness were something mysterious, something to be really proud of. It could be that that was the exact moment in which I began to be proud of quietness, too.

Real Life

Ten minutes later, Sap and I had walked around the back corner of the walkway, and paused there, both showing off to one another by ducking under the handrail, and hanging out in space.

"Sammy says his father hates being dragged down," said Sap. "He just *has* to hang loose. He didn't want Sammy, but Sammy's aunt got fed up with looking after him, because she had taken up with a new guy who didn't like kids, especially not boys." Sap had obviously been asking a lot of questions while I was off at Squintum's House. "His aunty just pushed him onto a plane without even letting on to his old man that Sam was on the way. Sam says she was frightened his father might just vanish, and that the Welfare people would find him and send him back to her . . . to the aunt, I mean. Or put him in a foster home. But his father was shacked up with Ginevra, and Ginevra liked Sammy—" Sap broke off suddenly. "Widdershins! He's coming round the house widdershins!" Sure enough, there was Sammy coming along the walkway toward us, but from the opposite side of the house, still carrying the basketball. "Perhaps he's a demon."

Sammy stopped at the corner, and leaned against the wall. Sap began to talk to him instead of me.

"Ginevra says she's made thousands of dollars!" she said. "But what's so great about smashing up cars?" She swung out halfway round one of the supporting steel posts. "Was she *married* to your father?"

"No way!" said Sammy. "They just hung out together."

"Did he crash cars, too?" asked Sap.

"He crashed everything, man," said Sammy. "Crash! Crash! Crash! I don't mind that he's split." He bounced the ball on the walkway. Bop! Bop!

Sap was longing to know exactly what was going on. She loved having things all named and sorted out so that she could tell other people about them.

"It's funny," she went on, watching Sammy. "Hero says nothing, and Ginevra says everything, but it all turns out the same way. Like, for instance, Ginny crashed our car, and there was this great fight. But now she's in there, talking about car crashing, just like it was some skookum-intelligent thing to do. That's spooky. And Hero does gardening for Miss Credence, this woman who lives in a huge house behind a big brick wall. (See those trees over there? Well, that's where Miss Credence hangs out.) And Hero goes in behind that wall, and never ever says one thing about what's on the other side. Not—one—thing! That's spooky too." She paused, but Sammy, though he looked out toward the green billow of the Credence forest, had nothing to say. Sap tried again. "Are you staying long?"

Sammy pulled a face and shrugged.

"Oh, yeah! Great!" cried Sap impatiently. "You're nearly as bad as Hero. I'd *die* if I couldn't talk and tell. I'd swell and swell and explode. Boom! Words and blood and guts falling down,

down, down . . . " She made a sprinkling gesture, arms stuck stiffly out in front of her, fingers wriggling, just like a little kid doing actions for a day-care song about rain.

"Doesn't she *ever* talk?" asked Sammy, looking at me. "Never?"

Sap couldn't resist giving him her theory. (Actually it was Annie's theory, but Sap had taken it over.)

"It's because Ginevra was always fighting with Annie and Mike. Everyone saying it wasn't their fault, whatever it was, and blaming everyone else. So! OK! All that yelling and blaming was like a karate chop inside Hero's brain. Wham!" She demonstrated with the edge of her hand against her own forehead, like an egg slicing its own top off.

"Shit," said Sammy, staring at me. "Weird!"

Sap watched Sammy watching me. Then she took another look at me herself, but proudly this time, as if she had accidentally invented me. Suddenly I wanted to escape from the double stare. Down below the walkway planks I could see that the window of the workroom was wide open. Athol often locked the door when he was working, but I felt certain I could swing down and slide into the study from above.

"Did you shift around with your father and Ginevra?" Sap was asking Sammy. "What about going to school?"

"Went to school when I lived with my cousins," Sammy said. But he wasn't interested in talking about himself right then. He was still staring at me as I lowered myself over the edge of the walkway. I stood on a steel crossbar, then stepped backward, groping with one foot for the windowsill.

"What are you doing?" yelled Sap. "You'll fall. You'll fall! Oh, no you won't," she added a moment later as, making myself thin, I successfully slid in under the glass in its cobwebby frame, stepped down onto a heavy, carved, wooden box, and from there to the floor. As I did this, I had the odd feeling that I was really practicing for something else, something I was planning to do some day but wouldn't let on about, not even to myself.

In those days, the study was a cramped room lined with book-shelves. Motley was curled up asleep in a bottom drawer that someone, probably Athol, had left open. She loved being boxed in. There was a narrow old couch along one wall, and I saw that someone, probably Mike, had dumped Sammy's pack on it, along with a blue sleeping bag. Sammy was being tidied into a room where there was no room to dance. I could see there wasn't much inside his pack. It had a floppy, collapsed look to it even though he hadn't unpacked anything, and I found myself won-dering if that ball he carried around with him was the only thing he truly owned.

Most of the desk was taken up with the computer and its key-board and screen. We had only one computer then, and it was busy nearly all the time. Annie used it at night and on weekends (it was compatible with the one she used at work), and Athol used it nearly all day, locking himself in after breakfast, coming out from time to time to make himself cups of coffee, then going back in again, carrying the coffee with a biscuit or two laid across the top of the mug. It wasn't that the study was forbidden to the rest of us, or anything like that. It was just that people working in there wanted to be on their own, listening for their own words, finding them, then fixing them in the computer's memory.

Coming in by the window made the study seem like a room in someone else's house. Books! Books! Books! Files! Files! Files! Motley looked up at me and mewed. She had a funny mew, for her mouth opened widely but only a tiny squeak struggled out into the world. I was glad that she was curled up, not stretched out, cozy not cold, and glad that she never went far from home.

Athol's notebooks were sitting beside the computer. Most of them were held tightly together by a rubber band, but one of them was sitting separate from the rest. I picked it up and opened it at random.

It wasn't what I expected. The page in front of me seemed to be set out like a play, and at the top of the page someone called Kate was speaking.

There's a big difference between getting things wrong and actually failing, she was saying. *A failed family falls to pieces around its mistakes. But we exploit ours . . . feed on them. We're vampires of disaster.*

This conversation, in big scrawly writing that almost filled the page, reminded me of something, but I couldn't work out what. Outside, I could hear voices—Sammy and Sap, bored with waiting for me, were shuffling along the walkway, probably going toward the front door.

I looked at the notebook once more. The next piece, written in red ballpoint pen, was something said by someone called Philip.

PHILIP: Slight complication in my chosen career. I'm held
    together by faith and

I knew how the sentence ended even before reading the end. I had heard Ginevra say those exact words at breakfast that morning.

There were soft steps in the hall. A hand fell on the door handle. I shut the notebook just before Athol himself came in and caught me in the act of spying. He was certainly surprised to see me there.

"Hello," he exclaimed. "How did you sneak past us?"

I listened carefully, and heard nothing but silence out in the house beyond.

"I came in by the window," I said at last.

My unused voice always surprised me. Whenever I did speak, I was always astonished to hear how *booming* I sounded. In my mind, my voice was as pure and clear as the voice of a bird. In the outside world it sounded more like a frog . . . a tuneful frog, but a frog all the same.

Real Life

Athol wasn't surprised or triumphant to hear me speak, and it wasn't just because I occasionally talked to him if we were on our own together. I spoke, and he listened in a drifting way, as if it were no big deal and he were really thinking of something else. It was because of his vague expression that I felt able to talk without giving too much of myself away.

"And so what do you think about it all?" he asked. "About Ginevra coming home, I mean?"

I asked him a question in return. "Who was David Ching?" Athol looked puzzled. "Ginevra said she wasn't as brilliant as David Ching." What I *really* wanted to ask him was how Philip and Kate, his notebook people, could possibly fit into New Historicism, or any sort of university work.

"David?" said Athol. "Davy Ching?" He sat down on the office stool and swung himself slowly around. "Were you listening in? Davy was in Ginevra's class at school and then went on to university at the same time as she did." As he revolved, I saw his nose, then his ear, then the back of his head.

"Was he her boyfriend or something?" I asked, as his nose came round again.

"No," said Athol. "It was just that Ginevra was always top of her class without any effort until Davy turned up in her seventh-form year, and by the end of the second year at university he was getting better marks than she was."

"Was she mad?" I asked, mostly to keep him talking. I thought I already knew the answer, but Athol's answers could be surprising, and he surprised me now.

"Not mad! Terrified!" he replied. "And of course *that* made her mad. The thing was, Davy *worked*. Worked hard! Like me. But Ginevra thought that having to work ruined everything. I reckon Mike and Annie had made a terrible mistake in thinking Ginevra wanted to be a clever girl (which was what they wanted for her, although they pretended they didn't). What Ginny really wanted was to be a *magician*. And, for a while back then, it seemed that she just might be one. I mean, everyone acted as if she was. Then Davy came along, caught her up, passed her and, bang! The magician was gone. Ginny was just another bright kid in a world full of bright kids, all catching up on her and more than one passing her. Bit of a comedown!"

"Was she jealous of him?" I asked. Athol frowned.

"I don't think she was . . . well, not much," he said at last. "She probably felt Annie had acted out this magical life in front of her, promising her that magic was possible but somehow keeping it all for herself. The thing is . . ." Athol looked at the edge of the desk, frowning and rubbing his thumb against it. "Why has she come home? Ginevra that is. It's not just a broken arm. There's something else."

"How do you know?" I suggested.

"I do know!" said Athol. "Trust me! And it can't be anything great, or she'd have told us all, straight off." Then he looked up at me, with his calm, fair face shining a little in the dim room, and took his notebook out of my hand. "Have you been reading my private research?"

"I didn't know it was secret," I said, probably looking guilty.

Athol leaned forward. His Cheshire cat smile was nowhere in sight. He pointed a finger at me. Right then I thought he looked threatening.

"I don't tell on you," he said. "Don't you tell on me. Not that you *do* tell, but, all the same, *don't!*"

I shook my head, and I meant it as a promise, but for the life of me I couldn't work out just what Philip and Kate had to do with anything, or what it was I had promised not to tell about.

Athol had turned back to look at the screen as if, even though it was completely empty, he could see the ghosts of words there. He hit the starting button and the computer began its warm-up. *Base memory*, I read. *Extended memory, dedicated memory.*

"Damn!" said Athol. "I won't be able to concentrate. I know it. Not today. Where have you been, anyway? Squintum's House?"

I touched the pocket where I thought I had put my Credence money, and had a jolt of panic, thinking I'd lost the envelope while scrambling about in the scaffolding. But then I remembered my other pocket, which I didn't use very often, and it was there, safe and sound, so I breathed again as I pulled it out to show Athol, unfolding the twenty-dollar note lovingly. Because of the Credence gardening work, I was rich. Richer than Athol, probably. As it turned out, I was quite a lot richer than I was supposed to be, because I was holding not one but two twenty-dollar notes. A second note had been folded up inside the first one.

"God!" said Athol, looking startled. "What do you have to do for that?"

"Garden and listen to stories," I said. "And take photographs!" I added, shivering to myself.

Although I knew immediately that I must give the extra money back again, I also felt, in a funny way, that the money was mine. It had been freely passed over to me in true life, and I'd earned it by taking that horrible photograph. Besides, the notes were so new and crisp, their folds coinciding so exactly, that it was as if they were both part of the same thing. If I didn't take that money back to Squintum's House at once, I might never be able to give it up.

True Life

Late that afternoon, early that evening, in fact, I went back to Squintum's House. I'd never been twice on the same day before.

The wind had dropped away and there were one or two people out for an evening walk, looking over hedges at other people's gardens and reading the graffiti on the Credence wall. But I was the only one who knew anything about what lay beyond those bricks, now that the other explorer, the ginger one, was dead.

None of the people I passed showed any interest in me and I wasn't interested in them. And yet I was sure someone was *watching* me. Someone's interest seemed to brush at my shoulder with every step I took. I looked behind me. Nothing! Then, at the Park Place corner, I swung round again, looking this way and that. Nothing! Nobody and nothing! Not even a seagull. I wondered if I might be watching myself in some way, saying, *Yes, there she goes! Jorinda taking wing! Going to Squintum's House for the second time on the same day. Going for the second time for the first time.*

There were lots of people in the park, some walking, runners jogging around the edge of it, and a crowd playing one of those games where two teams take turns hitting balls and running. But the playground was empty. I climbed the tree in the corner, ran along the top of the wall, in and out of the broken glass, edged out along my usual branch, making it curtsey under my weight, stepped onto another branch and came, at last, to my roadways through the trees. And up there, even though I'd come for a practical purpose, I turned, once more, just for a few minutes, into the wild girl of Squintum's forest . . . the one beyond names and human language, able to speak with animals and birds. I didn't know it then, but it was the last time the trees would ever work their spell on me. I would never be that wild child again. My true life was about to change, but after all, though it was true to me, that life had also been a dream.

In *The Jungle Book*, Mowgli is brought up by wolves and talks to wolves. There really have been wild children who have lived among animals, but no girl brought up among the trees would learn to sing or fly like a bird. In real life Mowgli would have been what they call a feral child, his wolfness his human ruin. No matter how closely I pressed myself into the magical life I had invented for myself, no matter how true I forced it to be, it had never yielded, not completely. Now, it was about to close down for ever.

I zigzagged backward and forward among the leaves, stepping lightly up, swinging down, then climbing as high as I could until I burst through the leaves, mouth open, to shout soundlessly at the sky, or maybe to breathe it in. Anyhow, I filled myself with happiness. It was only when I had somehow used up the happiness that I picked my way to the tree by the garden shed, stepped on to the sloping roof and then slid down the back where it was very close to the ground. And when I faced the house I saw something that I had never seen before. The front door of Squintum's House was open.

I can't tell you how mysterious that ordinary, open door suddenly seemed to be.

I had seen it open and close obediently behind Miss Credence, but I had never seen it held open before. I moved closer, tree by tree by tree. The light inside slapped a yellow oblong over the doorstep and out onto the gravel and grass. I slipped across the meadow that had once been a lawn. Grass heads brushed lightly against my knees, and then I was hesitating on the doorstep, looking through the shadows and along a lighted hall.

Miss Credence was hanging there. I could see the tilt of her hat quite plainly, and the folds in the hem of her cloak dangling well above the floor. And then, staring in dread, I made out that both hat and cloak were hanging empty.

A square of old carpet was spread on a chessboard floor, tiled in black and white. I could see an umbrella stand, and a great, looming piece of furniture . . . a mirror set in dusty wood, and wooden hooks from which dangled, not only Miss Credence's black cloak and hat, but other, ancient coats as well. I had a perfect excuse to call because I was returning the twenty dollars which Miss Credence had accidentally paid me. I was being honest. I knocked softly, and then knocked again, but nobody answered. No surprises there! I hadn't really intended Miss Credence to hear me. So I slipped through the door, which was propped open by a brass rooster, striding and crowing within a black iron frame, and into the long hall, hung with coats and set around with other doors. One of them was wide open, but the door directly in front of me at the far end of the hall was shut, and there beside it was another of the little square blisters . . . another code box, just like the other two. Another lock.

There was plenty to look at, however, without worrying about locked doors, or what might be behind them. And I was being looked at. The heads of two deer and a wild pig with tusks all gazed down at me with glass eyes. I noticed there was no cat's head. Not yet, anyway.

The hall was paneled with dark, rather dreary wood, and the coats dangling around the mirror looked like dry, dusty, discarded skins, or not even skins. Really, they looked more like people in a horror story, hung shriveling there for a hundred years.

On my left was a third door, which was closed, and on my right was the open door I've already mentioned, a double doorway in the shape of an arch through which I could see a huge table, a set of six chairs with curving backs, and, beyond these, enormous bulging leather armchairs with dull-colored cushions. On the wall were mounted heads of deer and sets of antlers, underlined by an old gun—*the* gun—laid horizontally on wooden brackets. Beside the gun hung a large sepia photograph in a heavy wooden frame—Professor Credence, smiling across a dead stag which was stretched out at his feet. He had raised its head by one of its antlers, twisting it so that it had to look at the camera, too. Earlier in the day, when I had taken her photograph, Miss Credence, I now saw, had copied her father's triumphant pose, but somehow her head had had the same twisted tilt to it as the head of the stag.

Over the fireplace hung a big oil painting, also of Professor Credence, looking out from under his black hat as if he were about to tell me something really important. His black cloak fell in straight folds around him. I stared at him for quite a long time. Then I turned and looked through an open door behind me into a kitchen, its sink piled with dirty dishes.

THE OTHER SIDE OF SILENCE

Suddenly, sound burst out all around me . . . a screaming gobble of sound that made me think of someone trying to strangle an animal. I didn't just start, I jumped, and, spinning round and round, tried to work out where that sound was coming from. It seemed to fall on me from every direction before stopping as suddenly as it had begun. After being frightened by that weird gobbling, the silence was even more frightening.

One corner of the room looked as if it were actually lived in. There was a window . . . one of those windows that stick out a little . . . a bow window. And in the pushed-out bit of the wall where the window was stood a card table with a book open on it, and several coffee cups clustered around the book. And it was not just the book and the coffee cups that made that corner look lively. The chair beside the table looked as if someone had just leapt up from it in the middle of reading and drinking coffee, and would be back at any moment. Steam rose from one of the cups.

Then the door in the hall that had been closed opened behind me. Miss Credence came through it, turning toward the sitting room while the door clicked itself shut once more.

"Jorinda!" she said, not sounding particularly pleased to see me. "Did you knock?"

But I was ready for her, and held out the twenty dollars. There is no one in the world who is not distracted by the sight of twenty dollars. "Don't you want it?" she asked, sounding puzzled. Then, suddenly catching on, her expression changed. Her eyes seemed to bulge forward from twin caves under her eyebrows to look, more or less, into mine. "Oh, *that's* what I did with it. I knew I'd lost some, but, even when you're careful, money just seems to dissolve. Well, thank you very much." But she didn't take the money from my outstretched hand.

I had half hoped she would say, "Keep it. I meant you to have it. It was a little present!" But instead she began looking around the room with a startled expression, almost as if she were the stranger there, not me.

"It's funny," she said at last, laughing and shaking her head, "the way it all looks worse whenever I have visitors."

She didn't sound at all like herself—not the self I knew in the garden. And she didn't look like herself, either. Her dry, garden voice had somehow become a gabbling one . . . her words came in rushes, connected by commas rather than full stops. "You know, it suddenly comes to me—I've actually been meaning to ask you for a while (and now seems to be the right time), how would you like to earn a little extra? . . . do a bit of housekeeping?" She glanced into the kitchen. "Washing up, for example. You could practice now while I make a cup of tea . . ."

I knew that washing those dishes would be dreadful, and I stood there wondering how to refuse her offer. But then, just as if I'd already agreed, Miss Credence took off in a rush of words that swept my silence in front of it.

"My grandfather built this house, you know," she began, still looking around her with that startled expression, as if she, too, were seeing it for the first time. "There's craftsmanship in this house, and beautiful wood, properly cured, it will be here a hundred years from now." She sounded as if she were rattling off a poem she'd learned by heart, ignoring all full stops. "My grandmother came here as a bride, and my father grew up here, just as

I did, in my turn. He was a professor, a world figure in the field of symbolic logic—everyone knows that, but he was a member of MENSA as well, and they take only the top two and a half percent, so of course it was a thrill for him when I became a member too, which I did, but years later." She stopped with a slight gasp, and, as I wondered what MENSA was, I felt something wrench inside me. The change that had begun earlier in the day was in full flood. In real life I'd had to be honest; I'd had to return that money. But in true life, whatever it was that had flowed from the house out into the garden, forcing Miss Credence to pose in front of me with a dead cat in one hand and a gun in the other, was somehow tugging me from the garden into the house. Standing in the doorway of her own kitchen, watching me trying to fill the sink with hot water from a tap that dribbled and choked, Miss Credence was still a storyteller of a sort, but I knew she wasn't in charge of the story anymore. The story was in charge of her.

And so, why was I here in Squintum's House when I really wanted to be at home? I don't belong in this story, I kept thinking over and over again. I don't have to give in to it. This is the last time I'll ever come here.

Miss Credence spoke in gushes while the tap hawked and spat like someone old and dirty and ill. The cupboard under the sink was filthy, and there was no detergent, only a square of yellow soap in an old-fashioned soap shaker, which was probably quite kind to the environment but perhaps a bit too kind. It did not look as if it had been used for ages. Anyhow, I began washing the dishes as thoroughly as I could, using a gray dish mop and some rusting steel wool. Miss Credence seemed to have lived for weeks on tomato sauce. There were two trays stacked with dishes, and I noticed that one of them had a white china cup on it, a cup with a lid and a sort of short spout. It wasn't a teapot of any kind. Really, it looked like the sort of thing a hospital might use for an invalid, and then I noticed that it actually had the name of the city hospital printed on it in red. Anyhow, as I clattered away, Miss Credence danced around behind me, pretending to straighten things, and chattering on, chattering on.

"I've never cared for housework." She paused, leaning in the kitchen doorway, apparently expecting me to be surprised.

"I know it's all different now, and women aren't tied to the kitchen the way they used to be, but someone has to do the housework . . . and the funny thing is that when my mother died, my father wanted . . . he just couldn't help it, poor man . . . he wanted *me* to take over here, though he and Clem Byrne (Dr. Clemence Byrne, that is . . . I always called him Clem) . . . well, they had always spoken as if women should be moving out into wider fields, taking their place in the arts and sciences."

Dr. Clemence Byrne, always called "Clem," was new to me. She'd mentioned her father from time to time, but I'd never heard her mention "Clem" before. But suddenly there he was, and for some reason he sounded serious.

Miss Credence dodged around me to plug in an old electric kettle with a cord that had a dangerous, frayed look about it. Then she picked up a huge teapot with a foot like a claw, which looked as if it might be made of silver. As she poured out the tea, Miss Credence ran on and on, while I struggled with the greasy plates under the piddling tap.

"People don't always appreciate the gifted person, do you find that? Is that why you don't talk? I'd understand it if that were the reason, you know, because my father just couldn't see that he'd always pushed me toward certain ideas, and then, well, I couldn't suddenly pretend they weren't there anymore. But that's what he wanted me to do . . . to become his mother in a way (of course, *she* had always spoiled him, what with him being the only son) or, perhaps, to turn into my own mother. Poor thing, she had never operated at our level, and he'd often pointed that out to me, so I can't think why he thought I'd be happy to turn into another version of her. And then later"—here she paused, her sentence hanging loose, looking as if she wasn't sure quite how to finish it. Then words filtered through to her once more, and she was off and away—"yes, later I inherited this house which I look on as a responsibility, although it *is* big for one person, and you can see I have a bit of trouble keeping things up. I mean, my grandfather, and even my father, had gardeners and cleaning women, but I can't afford anything like that now. The investments have almost all gone. I do sell something from time to time, a picture, perhaps. But I will *not* sell the land. Never! Mr. McInnery—he's my lawyer—*he* says I should subdivide, because there's a firm that wants to build a village of townhouses here, very select, of course. But I can't let that happen. I have to keep it all going."

I let one lot of water run away, and began to fill the sink again. The tap panted and hissed, then coughed and cleared its throat. Water burst out of it, stopped, and then burst out again.

"The tea's ready," said Miss Credence. She put two cups on a tray covered with a green cloth, crisscrossed with white lines. It reminded me of a lawn marked out for some sort of game. She opened the fridge, which did not light up, and took a white jug from it. "Sugar? Do you take sugar? I don't expect you do, and it's not good for you, that refined, white stuff. Leave those dishes to soak, and come with me. We'll go to the study. Then we can look out over the garden."

As I turned to follow her I saw the twenty dollars lying beside the old toaster where I had left it when I began doing the dishes. I did something then which I've never been able to understand, but I think it might have been something to do with the magic of money and the feeling that the twenty dollars somehow belonged to me. I picked it up, and carried it with me.

We went back along the hall, and for the first time I realized that I had not yet seen a stair in Squintum's House. Overhead, there was a second story, but there was no visible way of reaching it.

Miss Credence's study was the second study I had been in that day, and both rooms had a lot in common, with books, papers and pens spread around on top of a desk. The Squintum air felt lighter in the study, as if it had been allowed in and out a few times over the last ten years.

Two pictures hung side by side on the far wall. One showed a grave-looking man in academic clothes . . . a black gown with a light-colored hood, and a mortarboard. Professor Credence again, though this time he smiled an unexpectedly shy smile. His black university gown looked rather like his black cloak. He must have felt comfortable behind a fence of long, black folds. But by now I understood that Miss Credence was not only keeping the house going . . . she was keeping something of her father alive, as well.

The other picture showed a little girl with long hair trailing down her back, turning and smiling over her shoulder, as if someone out of the frame had just spoken her name. It wasn't a photograph. It was a painting, but not a good one. The child's face bulged on one side in a way that suggested mumps rather than the curve of a smile. It was the sort of painting that I should have been able to laugh at. However, as I stared up at the smiling child, I felt more frightened than I had felt at any time during the visit. Even the gobbling sound I had heard in the sitting room had not filled me with the horror I now felt as I stared at that picture.

Seeing me staring at the painting, Miss Credence glanced up at it, too.

"Rinda!" she said, smiling fondly at the mumpish face. "You've heard me speak of my daughter, Rinda. Not that I ever married, but then I was always unconventional. I painted that picture myself, but it doesn't do her justice, because she was a beautiful girl. Beautiful and clever. She went away, of course. This place is too small for beautiful, clever people . . . too *cramped*. They just have to fly, and we have to let them fly." Then she sort of *squinnied* at me. "Actually, she looks a little like you." She thrust her hand toward me. I jerked away, thinking she might be trying to grab me, and at that moment I didn't want to be touched, let along grabbed. But all Miss Credence was doing was indicating the twenty dollars I was still holding.

"You keep it," she said. "It's not a present (I can't afford presents), but you might as well take it now. Then you can come back tomorrow morning and do some housekeeping for me . . . tidying this study, for example."

Somehow, I couldn't refuse to take it. I was trapped by my own silence and the lure of an extra twenty dollars. All I wanted was to run out of the study, out of the house, out of the garden and into the city outside. I wanted to run home, to shut the gate and lock the door. But I held on to the twenty dollars, and knew that, by accepting it, I was promising to come back again. Nine dollars an hour . . . two more visits, three at the most. And then Miss Credence handed me a cup of tea, which turned out to be hot, but with a strange metallic taste under its heat. As I drank it, the pictures of Professor Credence and Rinda fixed their eyes on me. *Keep your distance,* he was saying, but her message was, *Follow me!*

At last, I finished that terrible tea. I was free to smile and nod at Miss Credence, just as I usually did, and to walk out of the open door into the garden, and just walking away made me wonder what I had been worrying about. Of course I was free to come and go. So I went freely, walking *under* the trees and through the gate, though feeling as if Professor Credence himself were watching me walk away. And as I reached our house I almost thought he was standing in the doorway watching me come home. But it was Ginevra, talking to Sammy, who was standing on the veranda, panting a little as if he had been running a race.

"Hello, working girl," Ginevra called, when she saw me. "Dinner's ready, and *I* made it tonight, so you'll love it. One-handed lasagna! You're just in time."

I was glad to be home and suddenly felt hungry. Immediately, the strange day seemed as if it were one of those dreams that fade as you begin to wake. I began to turn Squintum's House into real life, to remind myself how normal it really was. It was a house lived in by someone who, no matter how much she resisted the idea, worked in a post shop. And suppose she had shot one of the cats that preyed on her birds? Was it so terrible for someone who wanted her garden to be a wild sanctuary? Wasn't it all really ordinary?

No. I couldn't force it to be ordinary. There was the picture. The picture of Rinda. There had to be an explanation for that particular picture. Miss Credence had said it looked like me, but I knew it wasn't me and I knew it wasn't Rinda, either. It was Ginevra. There was no doubt about it, because I had often seen the photograph that painting had been copied from. We had only just come to live in Benallan and Ginevra had never lived there. And yet that picture of her as a smiling child was hanging in Miss Credence's house, and had been hanging there long enough to be welded to the wall with spiders' webs. There had to be a reason. But though I tried and tried, I just couldn't imagine what that reason might be.

Real Life

That night the television was brought out of the study, like a good dog being taken for a walk, so that we could watch the local news. Sure enough, there was an item on the conference, and there was Annie being asked to give her opinion. "See?" said Ginevra. "Nothing's changed. You're still at it."

"You'll notice I was only on for about thirty seconds," Annie said. "The ones they really wanted to talk to were the Australians. And you'll notice that, these days, interviewers are always trying to show my faults." And she looked, not hurt, exactly, but thoughtful. "They barely mention *Average-Wonderful*. They ask about Hero instead."

"It is strange though," said Ginevra. "Not talking at all."

"Do *you* think I might have pressured her into it?" Annie asked, looking over at me. "I *can't* have. I just couldn't do anything so far from my own ideas," she said at last. "Mind you, I can't blame people for growing bored with *Average-Wonderful*. I'm bored with it myself. I'd love to touch on a new mystery, but you can't just ring up and order one."

"Rest on your laurels. They must be really comfortable by now, and you might get a street named after you," said Ginevra. "Old Prof Credence did."

"Only because he died," said Sap.

"Wrong," cried Athol. "Both wrong. Credence Crescent was named after the professor's father. That house has been there for ages, and the crescent's been there for nearly as long. It's only about twenty years since Professor Credence shuffled off."

"It's not as long as that, is it?" Mike looked uncertain. "Isn't there a memorial to him in the university library?"

"They put up a plaque when he won that European award," said Annie. "Come to think of it, I don't know quite when he did die."

"Oh well, maybe he's still alive then," Athol said. "Hero probably knows him well, but never gets round to mentioning it."

"He must be dead," said Annie. "He'd be round about a hundred if he were alive. Ninety, anyway."

"Ninety's not impossible," said Ginevra. And then they talked about other things.

The next day was Sunday. And on Sunday, Rappie came round again, fussing over Ginevra and happy to find Annie at home. We piled into two cars, Mike's Peugeot and the old Volkswagen, which was supposed to be Annie's, and we all zoomed off over the hills for a picnic at the head of the harbor. We had a great day with no fights. Ghosts of the forest, and Squintum's House, and Miss Credence, and particularly that picture of Rinda, sometimes drifted through my head like advertisements for spooky films. And now Professor Credence was there too, somehow forming out of the smoke of his own black cigarette, smiling that shy smile. But, apart from these ghosts, Sunday was all real life—a Sunday of settling in with one another—with Ginevra, I mean, and with Sammy, too, when anyone remembered him. He sat on the edge of the family (no rapping, no hip-hop, and remembering to say "thank you"), and nothing strange or frightening happened at all.

— PART THREE —

Real Life

Back then I used to go to an alternative school—a small private school that was supposed to give me lots of individual attention. And teachers were great when it came to individual attention, great on reading and Maori studies, though they were too democratic about science and math, almost as if anyone's opinion was as good as anyone else's. People who really love math, people like Ginevra, say, mostly don't become schoolteachers. Of course they don't often T-bone cars, either.

I woke on Monday morning and did what I always did—blinked a few times, thought about school, rolled over, stretched, then rolled out of bed. And *then* I made for the kitchen to find myself something to eat.

In old books you read about children getting together for midnight feasts, but what I liked best was a stolen feast in the early-morning silence, with the light growing pinker and pinker around me. And, of course, on most fine mornings during this particular spring and summer, I'd leave notes on the kitchen blackboard saying *Gone to Squintum's House*, and set off down Edwin Street, no doubt dropping an *Old Fairy Tales* trail of toast or cracker crumbs behind me.

Once in the kitchen, I opened the fridge, drank orange juice straight from the carton, grabbed a piece of pizza and a couple of olives, and then moved on to the pantry, hunting for a big slice of applesauce cake that I knew had been there the night before. I wasn't going to take it all, just cut off a good sliver for myself. Well, there was the plate, but it was empty. Someone else had got in first. Athol was my main suspect because, although he sat around reading and smiling as if his mind were above the rest of us, Athol was a midnight food-thief, just as I was a morning one.

Back to bed, cakeless! But, as I left the kitchen, a slot of pinkish light sliced down between the curtains and fell on Sammy, slumped in my blue chair in front of my bookcase. Lying on his knee, fallen from limp fingers, was what was left of the applesauce cake. He was fully dressed, even to his baseball cap, but he was sound asleep. Motley was sleeping, too, in the chair opposite, but she was curled up tightly whereas Sammy was stretched out. She opened her eyes into little slits, staring across her own tail, just checking. The patch of ginger on her head reminded me of that other cat, and I couldn't stop myself from wondering if, somewhere, a family had called out for him the night before, and the night before *that*, worried and sad when he hadn't come running.

Sammy slept on while I looked at him sourly. I did not want him there, eating my early-morning cake and sitting in my own blue chair, with my own bookcase behind him. But then nobody, except Ginevra, really wanted Sammy, not even his own father. We Rappers were just being nice to him for Ginevra's sake. And then, as if the slot of light were acting as a pointer, I noticed a little clean mark on his cheek. The light turned it silver. Some slug of sadness had crawled there not long ago. Something about the way he was lying propped in the blue chair reminded me in a funny way of the picture of the Sleeping Beauty in *Old Fairy Tales*. The illustrator isn't named, but he or she has drawn the princess not lying flat but sunk back into great blue cushions. Carefully and quietly, I squatted down beside the chair, pulled out the book, and carried it over to the kitchen table just to check up on my memory of the picture. I was running my finger down the list of pictures in the front of the book when I saw something that put all Sleeping Beauties, male or female, right out of my mind. My eye caught the name *Jorinda*.

I slammed the book shut. Sammy jumped as if he had heard distant gunfire, but he did not wake. Now, looking back, I think of him, accidentally asleep in the blue chair, packed in tightly but with a great space around him, not knowing the passwords to get out of that space, and nobody else knowing the passwords to get in. For our house, which seemed so safe to me, and even to Ginevra, was a place that was not true for Sammy, not even properly real, full of eyes glancing at him without any fondness, and jokes with last lines he couldn't possibly understand.

Even before I was back in bed I knew Squintum's House had turned into a sore place in my thoughts, like some bruise or scratch that you can't stop touching, just to check on how sore it really is. Going to sleep the night before I had kept bringing the picture of Squintum's House into my mind, trying to take it by surprise to see how I felt about it, and then quickly pushing it away again. I climbed into bed, turned on my bedside light and opened *Old Fairy Tales* for the second time that morning.

The story was called *Jorinda and Joringel* and when I saw it I could remember reading it a long time ago. Somehow it isn't one of the fairy tales that anyone really recalls, but it was there in the book all the time. Jorinda was a girl and Joringel was a young man. This is how the story began:

There was once an old castle in the middle of a forest and in it lived a witch who could call wild beasts and birds to her door. Then she killed them and roasted them. If any traveler came within a hundred paces of the castle she stole his power to move, and he just had to stand still until she allowed him to go free. But whenever an innocent maiden came within the circle, she changed her into a bird and shut her up in a wickerwork cage, and carried the cage to a room in the castle. She had about seven thousand cages of rare birds in that room.

Contact! Somewhere in my head all sorts of wheels and cogs began to spin and engage, pushing one another round and round. Miss Credence must have read this story when she was a child, and it had been like a turning cogwheel pushing *other* wheels in *her* head. Its energy had flowed from wheel to wheel (that's how stories worked for me, too), and Miss Credence had produced a story that was all her own. In the Grimms' fairy tale Jorinda was turned into a bird, until Joringel freed her from enchantment. Then the story ended. But Miss Credence's tale somehow suggested what had happened *after* the end. It turned out that Jorinda could never be set free. Bird nature had become part of her nature for ever. So she flew away from Joringel, back to the trees, back to the birds, and to the struggle against—not the witch, but the witch's son and heir, against Nocturno. The two stories, old and new, melted into one another, and into me, too. It was as if, because I was hesitating to go to Squintum's House, Squintum's House had somehow come to me . . . true life was swallowing real life in great, greedy gulps and taking its place. I felt the shadow of its huge maw fall across me.

It was a great relief to hear Mike begin moving around out in the kitchen about ten minutes later, to feel real family life rushing in, strong enough to keep me real, too.

Real Life

I got up for the second time that morning, and went down the hall holding *Old Fairy Tales* under my arm, past Athol's door, past the study, only to meet Annie coming out of the bathroom. She looked pale and damp and, for some reason, just not too well.

"Hero!" she said in a distracted voice. "Why aren't you off gardening?"

I smiled and shook my head, gave her a little hug with my bookless arm, and went into the dining room.

And then everyone came and went having breakfast, getting dressed, talking, arguing and joking (not me, but the others). We were almost used to having Ginevra home again by now, but we flowed around Sammy. And Annie and Ginevra were still being so careful with one another that I think it made us all uncomfortable. Ginevra's damaged face was a different color every morning. By now the swelling around her eye had gone down, but the color had darkened into bluish blacks and purples with a lurid yellow edge creeping back toward her ear and down her neck.

Driven out from my usual place, I sat at the end of the table watching them all. Athol was right. Once you knew there was something Ginevra was hesitating to tell, you could feel it on the edge of every other thing she had to say . . . words coming to the tip of her tongue only to be swallowed again. Once, when Mike was in the kitchen and Annie was in her bedroom putting on a university face, and Sap was searching for some homework she said she had done, Athol leaned over the table and spoke to Ginevra in a soft voice.

"What *is* it? Spit it out!"

"I will when I'm ready," she answered.

"I'll tell you something," said Athol, "in case it makes you feel better. I've got a confession to make, too."

Ginevra looked him over as if he were a mathematical puzzle. "Just give me a clue," she said.

"I gave you a clue the other day, but nobody was listening," said Athol. "Anyhow, if you tell your secret, then I'll tell mine. Scout's honor!"

"You don't fool me," said Ginevra. "I know you've never been a Scout. You probably don't have any bloody secret."

Sap came bouncing into the room

"What are you hugger-muggering about?" she asked suspiciously.

"We're not hugger-muggering," said Ginevra. "Because you shout all the time you think everyone else whispers." She looked at Athol. "I'll think about it," she said.

Sap and I biked to school together, but when I turned off Benallan Drive toward my school, she went on to hers. My school was called Kotoku House. Sending me there was really against Mike's principles. He had to admit, however, that even though the state school, Benallan Primary School, was what was called a "good" school, it just didn't have a lot of time for anyone with peculiar problems, and I counted as a peculiar problem—a problem to other people, that is, not to myself. Kotoku House was tiny . . . there were only about fifty pupils, a group of parent-helpers who worked for nothing, and two main teachers who were actually paid (though not very much, because the school wasn't rich, and they taught out of idealism). They were really dedicated, which they had to be because, though I was the quietest kid in the school, I wasn't the only one who had been sent there out of somebody's despair.

All morning I worked in silence, as I always did. No one could tell that I was locked in by names and memories and guesses—that Squintum's House invisibly caged me.

During my first term at Kotoku House, the teachers, Coralie and Peter (they liked to be called by their first names), were patient and understanding. But after a while I could tell that my silence hurt their feelings. They had been so sure that *they* would solve my problems, both through kindness, and through seeing the world in the right way. At school, however, it was as if I *couldn't* talk. I listened and wrote and read and did all the creative things they set for the kids to do, and every so often Coralie and Peter, or Bruce, my counselor from the psychological services, would try to work with me—just me—although deep down I knew they'd all given up.

I've seen Bruce's reports. I used to whip into the study, in the days before Athol started locking the door, and read what Mike left on the desk, just as I had read Athol's notebook on Saturday morning. If you don't ask questions you don't get answers, so you often have to find things out by spying.

The reports said that I was *aphasic voluntaria*. . . . blah! blah! blah! My sort of not-speaking was first called that in 1877. It mostly occurs between the ages of five and seven years, and it mostly responds to treatment. But watch out if it doesn't, because the problem becomes more intractable over time. At least, that is what it said in one report, which Mike and Annie probably still have filed away in the cupboards somewhere. In general, experts think it is caused by some trauma such as change of residence, illness, mouth injury, or a family upheaval. It can occur in "a family environment that promotes shyness." I mean, suppose you're a little kid and there's something going on in your family that suppresses speech (like people talking over you all the time), well, you may just decide to stop talking altogether. And that's what most people thought had happened to me. They thought that I had grown up at a time when everyone else in the family, mainly Annie and Ginevra, had been shouting and saying hard things to one another or about one another, and this had made me decide, secretly, that talking was too dangerous to be worthwhile. I'd always been quiet, but soon after Ginevra left home I stopped talking altogether, and they believed my first silences had turned into what they called a speech phobia. The theory was that I was avoiding speaking because I thought of talking as a sort of pain.

One counselor recommended *the utilization of a treatment strategy that acknowledges the individual situation of the subject.* (Me, that is. *I* was the subject.) He said that he had tried what he called *positive reinforcement of verbal behavior* in the beginning . . . which meant that he made a huge fuss of me if I accidentally said anything, no matter how silly it was. At my state school there was a time when I had had a special chart, and was given ticks and gold stars for every word I said. Apparently this sometimes works with kids who have stopped talking, but it didn't work with me. I just grew quieter and quieter, then totally silent, except in one environment, which in report language meant that I sometimes talked to Athol. After this they tried what was called *fading procedure*. For instance, if ever Mike or Annie heard me talking to Athol, they would come into the room, accidentally-on-purpose, just wandering in, pretending to be tidying up or looking for something they'd lost, but hoping that I would include them without really noticing I was doing it. This is another thing that apparently works sometimes. There are kids like me who begin talking in a week or two—*post-experimental increases in verbal response to teachers and peers*. There are some kids who progress to *speaking spontaneously to peers and adults in various situations*. But no matter what the counselor and other experts did, I wouldn't speak, not to kind teachers, not to peers, only occasionally, secretly, to Athol. By now, everyone was resigned to it, even at Kotoku House.

"What am I being punished for?" I once heard Annie say. "I've loved my children, and I've *wanted* them to be themselves."

But, for me, being myself meant being silent. "I suppose all parents push their kids in some direction," Annie had said. "But have I ever—ever *once*—stopped my children from being themselves? Have I?" Mike had no answers to this. No one had.

When I arrived home on Monday afternoon the house was empty, except for Mike that is. It seemed Ginevra had taken off with Sammy for a prowl around Benallan. More of a limp than a prowl, Mike added. Annie was at the university, talking to a group of students about their essays; Sap had stayed on after school because she was on the school swimming team and they were having a coaching session.

97

"Just you and me," Mike said. I grinned, and went to the fridge. I was going to get a scoop of ice cream, but the ice cream container was empty.

"Sammy ate the last of it," said Mike. "Never mind! I'm on my way to the supermarket to get some more. Want to come?"

So we set off together, walking to the Benallan Shopping Center which was a couple of blocks away. Mike is a skillful shopper. It doesn't sound much to say about anyone, but good shopping *is* a skill, and I reckon it can even become a bit of an art. Anyhow, Mike always pretended it was a great chore, but everyone knew he enjoyed it—well, everyone except Rappie, of course! The sight of Mike preparing for a run through the supermarket set her teeth on edge. "To think I supported you through university for this," she would say.

Mike was well prepared. He had been through current books of supermarket discount coupons, and had checked them against the two lists stuck on the fridge door with magnets. Coupons for things we *did* want, and for things we *might* want, and for store-cupboard things, were all cut out and held together with a paper clip. At the supermarket we would grab a cart, work our way through fruit and vegetables to pet food, then on through household hardware, only to bounce off the cheese-and-yogurt refrigerators into the next aisle—household cleaners and cosmetics. Arriving at ice cream and frozen peas, we would hesitate, then veer past the biscuits to the shelves of bread, and so on and so on, with Mike consulting his list every step of the way, reading labels (so that he knew exactly which cleaners were the greenest, and how much food coloring there was in which food and all that sort of thing), and shuffling the coupons as if they were a winning hand in a game of poker. Occasionally he would buy a lotto ticket. Annie really disapproves of gambling, but Mike says she wouldn't turn down a million dollars if ever he was lucky, and anyway, it's a state lottery, and part of the money goes to the Arts Council.

He bought a ticket on this particular day. "It's been an exceptional weekend," he said. "We'll see if we can't make it a winner."

After the supermarket we had to go into the post shop. Annie writes a lot of articles that fit into odd-size envelopes, which can't just be dropped into the box at the door. Post shop bound, we pushed along the Benallan Shopping Center sidewalks, and past a shop that sold electrical goods . . . washing machines, microwave ovens, tape decks and so on. The window was full of television sets, and every single screen was showing the same dramatic scenes from *Pharazyn Towers.*

Everyone talked about *Pharazyn Towers* at school, and posters advertising women's magazines promised revelations about the love lives of the stars, along with gossip about the Royal Family, so even though I'd never actually seen a whole episode, I knew that the thin, glamorous woman gesturing and mouthing over and over again in the shop window, was wicked Athelie Pharazyn, trying to ruin the life of Kate, who was in love with Oliver, who was the nephew of Philip (the man Athelie passionately desired, but who didn't fancy her). As we came up to the window, my feet wandered a little off course, and I came to a standstill. Mike stopped as well, and we both stared at wicked Athelie, sneering and laughing, and at Kate, weeping, pleading, and fluttering backward and forward.

And then Mike pulled himself together and hurried on, sweeping me out of the power of a soap opera, and into the safe, sensible post shop. There, poised behind the counter, was Miss Credence (the Monday-afternoon-post-shop version, real not true), wearing a moss green twinset and her silver locket, smiling her dry smile, and giving no suggestion, not the slightest, that she spent her early mornings stalking through a forest, wearing her father's cloak and hat, and shooting cats with his gun.

Mike bought stamps from her and asked for a receipt because Annie charges the cost of stamps against tax. Some post offices print out the receipts, but not the Benallan branch. Miss Credence had to write it out by hand.

"How's the garden?" he asked, as Miss Credence scribbled away.

"I don't know what I'd do without her," Miss Credence replied. "I've even asked her to tidy my study . . . it's a real mess. My own fault, mind you! All my office-cleaning energy goes into keeping *this* one in order."

She looked directly at me, and the gaze from her straight eye seemed to pin us, secretly, together. Everything she said sounded so *ordinary*, just everyday words coming across the post office counter. All the same, that twinset was a disguise. The person wearing it was a false figure carefully invented by a Miss Credence who was never actually seen in the streets of Benallan.

"What happened to you this morning?" she asked me, and added playfully, "Don't forget! I've paid you in advance."

"Hello," said a voice behind us, and, suddenly, there was Ginevra. "Fancy meeting you! Sammy and I might grab a lift.

We've walked our feet off around this fashionable part of the world."

"Your luck's out. We walked too," said Mike. He looked over at Miss Credence. "This is my oldest daughter, Ginevra, home for a while. Ginevra, this is Miss Credence, Hero's employer."

Ginevra grinned cheerfully at Miss Credence.

"Home for a visit?" Miss Credence asked politely.

"Resting between jobs," said Ginevra, and laughed.

"We should have asked her if her father really *is* dead," said Ginevra as we left the post shop, not knowing what strange ideas she was giving me. And then we saw Sammy.

At home Sammy looked uneasy and out of place, but here he actually looked unreliable . . . well, more than unreliable. In the trendy Benallan Shopping Center, with its parking lot full of expensive cars, Sammy looked totally suspect.

He was standing outside a sports shop, staring at a display of shoes in the doorway. They were all Nike or Adidas—the sort of shoes that get stolen at school, even at schools like Kotoku House. The woman in the shop certainly thought this when she looked out and saw Sammy standing there in his great sloppy T-shirt and shorts, his hair shaved up the sides but spraying out in ringlets on the top. Out she came, right onto the sidewalk, and said something to him. We couldn't hear her words, but her voice was sharp. Sammy threw up his hands to show they were empty, and took a step back from her.

Ginevra took off like a rocket.

"Leave him alone," she yelled as she ran. "Leave him alone!"

The woman spun round, and then began trying to tell Ginevra

how many pairs of shoes they lost through shoplifting, but Ginevra was already shouting that Sammy was entitled to look at things without being insulted, while Sammy rolled his eyes in embarrassment, muttering, "Forget it! Hey! Forget it! Oh, shit!" The woman stared wildly past Ginevra—who sounded Benallanish but must have looked, to her, like something from a horror film—and she recognized Mike. "Mr. Rapper," she cried. "Do tell her—please explain that I just have to look after the interests of the shop."

Some Benallanites were scurrying past us with remote, good-taste expressions on their faces, anxious not to be caught up in someone else's gross story. But others, the ones at a bit of a distance, couldn't help watching us with interest, as if we ourselves were on television in a shop window.

"Sammy belongs with us, Mrs. Harley," Mike began.

"He doesn't," yelled Ginevra, turning on Mike now. "He bloody well belongs to himself. He doesn't need you to say he's OK. He *is* OK."

"But how am I to know?" Mrs. Harley replied in a pitiful, bleating, private-school voice. "We lose hundreds of dollars' worth of shoes, and it's mostly these young people who are responsible . . . "

"Why do you put your bloody shoes out on the street, then?" demanded Ginevra. "And why pick on Sammy? It's because he's *brown*, isn't it? Not very brown, just a bit brown! That's enough, isn't it, just being slightly darker than everybody else."

"Shut up! Shut up!" Sammy was saying. "Get off my case." But nobody was listening to him, least of all Ginevra.

"I'm sorry," Mrs. Harley began saying, turning scarlet under her bleached hair. "How was I to know? I'm sorry."

Suddenly, Ginevra stopped, but not because she was accepting the apology, or anything. Suddenly, something else, something invisible, was demanding all her attention. When she spoke again, her voice sounded distant, almost dreamy.

"Well, you should be sorry," she began, then stopped again. Something was wrong with her. I could see her swallowing, and I thought she might be trying to stop herself crying.

"Hey!" said Sammy, staring at her anxiously. "It's OK. It's cool!" He looked over at Mrs. Harley. "No big deal."

"No!" said Ginevra, turning on Sammy now, trying hard to find her way back to her first fury. "Don't ever, *ever* let any Ben-allan-type gang push you around!" But I was watching her at the exact moment when whatever it was she was fighting against took over. Her eyes lost their focus and ferocity; her gaze drifted. "You've got to be *staunch*," said Ginevra, using gang language, but with her voice retreating. She swayed, and then dropped to the ground like something used up and thrown away. I'd never seen anything like it. I thought she was dead.

True Life

I set out for Squintum's House in the light, long, late-summer evening, leaving the great family song—one solo interrupting another and sudden choruses interrupting the solos—behind me. I left Ginevra sitting in a chair, and saying over and over again, "God, I feel so stupid!" and Sap, who was home from the swimming pool with her hair dried into rats' tails, asking her if she'd had a fit.

"I just came over all funny," said Ginevra. "I suppose the crash must have left all sorts of shock effects."

Her faint in the Benallan Shopping Center had lasted less than a minute. Mrs. Harley had dashed into the back of the shop and brought her a glass of water, spilling most of it because her hand was shaking so badly. People clustered around, some offering to help, and others just watching with interest. Mrs. Harley kept on saying, "It wasn't my fault." She was really upset.

"I can walk," Ginevra said at last. "Let's go home." Mike and Sammy each took one of her arms. "I can walk," she cried, but Mrs. Harley insisted on calling a taxi. The Bretts, drawing out lead-headed nails like carpenter-dentists, and prizing off sheets of iron, had looked down with fascination as Mike and Sammy helped Ginevra up the steps.

"Everything OK?" Colin called down from the roof, trying to find out just what was happening in the latest thrilling episode.

"Fine," said Mike, rather irritably, and the Bretts immediately began working twice as hard as before. To the sound of feet on the walkway and the screech of nails being prized out of iron and timber, we propped Ginevra in my blue chair.

"I'll make a cup of tea," offered Sammy, still looking alarmed. I went into the kitchen with him to point out where we kept tea bags and so on, and we wove around one another, putting the kettle on to boil and warming the teapot.

"Man, has she got *attitude!*" said Sammy, meaning Ginevra.

"Didn't she thrash in? Slam dunk!" He talked quite a lot, but in his own language, which I had to guess at. Anyhow, we made tea together, feeling quite friendly, I think, brought together by drama, danger and disaster. Then we fussed over Ginevra, putting cushions round her. Every now and then, looking up through the skylights, I saw the dark shadows of Brett feet walking by, and knew how easily they could listen to our private story from up there.

Dinner was going to be late, and I suddenly thought of Miss Credence, and of the way she had casually reminded me she was paying me in advance—not being nasty about it, but definitely meaning me to take notice. I didn't want that money now. I wished I had given it back. But I hadn't. I had accepted it, which meant I had no choice. I had to go back to Squintum's House and finish twenty dollars' worth of work for her. Once that was done, I thought, I would never go back again, and in time I would break free from the spell, not because some Joringel would appear to touch me with a blood-red flower and rescue me, but because I was my own magician and had the power to rescue myself. So I left Sammy and Sap to help Mike cook dinner, and walked toward Squintum's House.

Usually, as I moved into Credence Crescent, I felt myself grow more *concentrated*, as if I were super-real, while the world around me became somehow *finer*, almost transparent, as if I might be able to walk right through walls rather than climb over them. But this time there was no change, either in the world or in me. Trailing my fingers over the bricks of the Credence wall, I read the graffiti, and saw how someone with a spray can had struck out the word KILL in KILL THE PUNKS and printed the word

HUG in its place. I watched the gateposts as I came toward them, and even touched the rusty chain that held them together, thinking it wasn't the sort of protection you could depend on. That secret wildness I felt at the heart of things whenever I was on my own was still there, but this time it didn't reach out to take me in. This time I was shut out.

And, once again, I felt that someone was watching me, wanting to know where I was off to, and why. I looked back over my shoulder every now and then, but I couldn't see anyone spying on me. I didn't really expect to, in spite of that spooky feeling tapping at my shoulder.

Then I was inside the secret garden once more. I walked four trees down the avenue of lindens to a tree I knew I could easily climb, and I climbed it. I picked my way through the familiar branches, watching the house come toward me, staring with its white eye, then I slid down on to the garden shed roof, and onto the ground.

The front door was open, just as it had been on Saturday evening. I knocked, but, once again, no one answered. I walked into the hall, and looked at the dusty skins hanging from the hooks, and the animal heads staring at me from glass eyes on which dust lay like a film of death. Then I moved on past the study, and stared at the third door, the one that was closed and coded and locked.

Waking that morning, and on my way to school, I had imagined it might be the study with its two pictures that was alarming me, but now I realized that, at the back of my mind, I had also been remembering this locked door and the metallic blister under the little grille. Everyone knows that people need security systems outside a house. But who would need one inside? I thought about that tray with the invalid cup on it, and then about my family discussing whether Professor Credence really *was* dead. Somehow or other, a story seemed to be struggling into existence.

I went into the sitting room and stopped in surprise. There was a whole lot of smashed china in the middle of the floor . . . not just one or two plates, but cups and saucers, too—a cream jug and a big serving dish. I felt my forehead wrinkling in puzzlement and dismay.

But just then Miss Credence popped out of the kitchen. "There you are," she said cheerfully. "Good. I'll be glad of the help. I suppose it seems to you that I could keep the house in much better order, but my mother used to do all that sort of thing. She was a good housekeeper and took a lot of pride in having things nice, and my father wanted me to be free of all that, bless him; he wanted me to concentrate on more imaginative things—until my mother died, that is, because, when it came to the point, he wanted things around him to be orderly." She glanced down at the pile of broken china and seemed as surprised as I was to see it there. Yet she offered no explanation, and her chatter flowed on quite cheerfully as she led me back into the hall and toward the study. " 'Well,' I said to him, 'you always said you wanted me to fly. You brought me up to have a mind above housework. Get someone else to tidy up after you.' But he was already ill, and he didn't want a stranger wandering around the house, and, looking back, I can understand that now, though I don't mind *you* being here, of course. We *do* seem to have a special understanding, don't we?" She paused, not to listen to any answer I might suddenly make, but simply to take breath.

"We'll start in here, because that's where I do most of my work, I mean my *true* work, because I don't count the job at the post shop, that's just to keep money coming in, although I'm the only woman in the city to have full charge of a branch—and the Benallan branch, too, which means I'm dealing with a lot of businesspeople, as well as university people like your mother. It's a way of flying, I suppose."

The top of the desk was covered with piles of paper, each one weighed down with some small object—a brass elephant, a speckled stone, a candlestick and so on. She'd talked about her work, but anyone could tell these papers hadn't been lifted or sorted for ages. It wasn't just the dust. Paper has a way of settling down on itself if nobody disturbs it.

From the wall, Professor Credence stared at me, smiling shyly, and the dreadful painted Ginevra, who was called "Rinda" in this house, looked back over her shoulder. But I felt certain there had never been any such person as Rinda. Miss Credence had invented a daughter for herself, mixed up out of longing and loneliness, and had given her the face of a child who was famous for saying clever things.

"I think you should begin with the bookcases," said Miss Credence. "Take the books out in order, and put them back in order (do be very careful about that, they've been arranged as I want them arranged), then wipe the shelves, rub furniture oil into them, and put the books back exactly as they were. Of course, I don't need to tell you that you mustn't read anything on the desk." (Her voice, which had been gabbling rapidly, slowed down, becoming very deliberate, as she said this, and she looked at me sternly.) "It's all private, but I know I can trust you," she added. It sounded quite straightforward, and yet somehow or other she managed to suggest we were really sharing a secret of some kind.

But there was no secret. Or, if there was, I had no idea what it might be.

Suddenly, that *gobbling* sound I had first heard in the sitting room burst out of the air around me.

"It's the pipes," cried Miss Credence, and thumped the wall by the door, commanding any pipes that might be behind the stained wood to behave themselves. "They get air bubbles in them. Let's run off a bucket of water, and that'll get the system flowing freely again. And we'll get dusters and the polish while we're about it. Then you'll be able to get down to good, honest work." She smiled indulgently, as if she were offering me something that I had been longing for.

We went through to the kitchen. The green bucket she dragged out for me hadn't been used for ages. The rags hanging over its handle were as hard and gray as wood. Miss Credence picked up a new bottle of furniture oil, the same sort that Mike bought at his supermarket, and read the label carefully, as if it held dangerous medicine.

"Rub well!" she announced. "You'll need a soft, dry cloth." She pulled a tea towel from the rack and passed it over to me. "Take this. It's an old one." The gobbling sound came again. "Those pipes!" she said, and thumped on the wall, but she didn't fool me. This sound was definitely in the air, not in the wall.

We half-filled the bucket from the dribbling tap over the kitchen sink, and I followed her back to the study.

"Well, I'll leave you to it," she said, and then stood, wavering and frowning, her mouth opening and closing. "Be careful with everything on the *desk*," she said at last, speaking with the same curious deliberation I had heard in her voice before. "Everything's set out in special piles." And then she stared hard at the top of the desk, frowning at something in such a way she seemed to be pointing it out with her eyebrows. At last, she gave a quick smile, slid round the door and closed it softly behind her, just as if I were asleep and mustn't be wakened.

Something scratched at a window, one corner of which was draped with cobwebs as dense as grayish rags. A tree on the other side of the glass stretched out a twig toward me, beckoning me back to a safe place among the leaves. But it was much too late for that. I had come down from the trees. The story I was part of now was even more famous than *The Jungle Book*. Everyone knew it, even people who didn't read. It was the tale of a bride who was allowed to go anywhere in a house except for one forbidden room. Of course, in the end, she couldn't resist going into that room, and found other brides, all strangled, hanging there. The name of the story is *Bluebeard*.

True Life

Annie talks rather impatiently of the way her grandmother taught her to hang out washing and dry dishes. "She always behaved as if hanging out washing was a special skill, but I suppose if you don't have the chance to do anything else you somehow make a skill out of it," I once heard her say. "Whoa!" cried Mike indignantly, because for years he was the one who'd done most of the washing around our house. "Did your granny grow up with a washing machine and spin dryer? Getting washing dry probably *was* a skill in those days."

The thing is that no one in our family had ever been taught to admire that particular sort of skill. Housework doesn't have your name on it, the way books do. It doesn't hold still long enough to be worth signing, or to count as art.

So, when I began doing what Miss Credence had told me to do, I felt unnatural and clumsy. The books were tightly jammed together on the shelves. No one had moved them for ages. The covers weren't exactly stuck together, but they parted regretfully, like fairy-tale lovers being pulled out of a kiss. Dust was thick along their tops—thick enough to drift and rise around me as I blew it away or banged the books together. The first bookcase took me ages to tidy properly, and the books weren't all that interesting, either. I certainly wasn't tempted to read any of them.

The first few shelves were all bound copies of a magazine, *Philosophy and Literature*—years and years of *Philosophy and Literature,* wrapped in films of dust. I opened one copy and saw an article, "Explorations of Self Through Narrative," or something like that. That interested me. I mean, narrative is another name for story, and I was always trying to match my own life with one story or another. I wasn't the only one either. By now I was beginning to understand that Miss Credence had once wanted to be a bird girl—to break out of the cage and fly. She had used the Grimms' fairy tale as a jumping-off place, rather as I had used *The Jungle Book*. Anyhow, I finished the first bookcase, and then rather hurried over the next one. I don't suppose cleaning the study was any grittier or grubbier than gardening, but it felt *dirtier*, and I found myself longing for a vacuum cleaner, which puts a safe distance between dirt and the person doing the cleaning.

At last, I took a break, and wandered over to the desk. There, among the piles of paper, propped against a jam jar filled with pens, was a book with a clasp held open by a stone, and not an ordinary stone, either. A fossil! And, though I wasn't clever at cleaning shelves, I actually knew something about fossils. This creature, once living and now turned to stone, was a trilobite. Millions of years ago trilobites had ruled the world.

The book was one of those birthday books, carefully opened at a page early in September. There before me was an entry for Miss Credence's birthday, and her full name, Miranda Star Credence, written in elegant, old-fashioned writing. Just for a moment, even though I'd never heard her full name before, I seemed to recognize it, and then I realized that what I was really recognizing was not the name but the date—0809—which was also the code for the Credence Crescent gate. It wasn't particularly clever of me to recognize it. Miss Credence had written it out at the top of the page, zeros and all. And in spite of everything, in spite of the fact that just being there in that study, watched by the pictures of Professor Credence and Ginevra-turned-into-Rinda, was making me feel so spooky, I began to grow inquisitive, quite against my own will. I remembered Miss Credence's crooked forefinger pecking twice at the first key on the code panel at the front door of the house, and, since the house and the gate had the same kind of code panel, I now knew that that first key must have been "1." The house code must begin with two ones, then . . . perhaps the eleventh of something. Trying to pretend to myself that I was checking up carelessly, I flicked over to the 11th of January. Nothing! So then I flipped from month to month, from one 11th to the next, and suddenly there it was on the 11th of August. At the top of the page, written in pencil, were the numbers 1108, and below was another birthday entry . . . Conrad Hilary Credence, born 1906. There was no date for his death.

Curiosity arched up in me, sticking out its claws as it grew. Very quietly, I left the study and, after looking briefly at that other closed door at the back of the hall, I slipped out through the front door, clicking it shut behind me. After all, I could always knock or ring to be let in again. Miss Credence could ask who was knocking at her door. "Lift up the latch and walk in," she would tell me. Not that I would answer. I'd just ring and keep on ringing. In the end she would have to let me in again.

I tried the code 1108. There was a soft click. I pushed the door, and it opened easily. I closed it, and tried it all over again. Then I went back to the study and the bookcases, excited, though I wasn't sure why. It wasn't as if I had ever planned to break into Squintum's House, was it?

More bound copies of magazines! More dust! My cleaning and polishing did make a difference, though. The bookcases began to look unexpectedly grand. These books, all the same size and thickness, were so *precise* on the shelves.

By now a pattern was forming inside my head, and after a while I couldn't stop myself. Back I went to the birthday book and flicked past one empty page after another. I came to the end of December and began all over again. This time I found what I was looking for, though it took me by surprise when I did find it. There it was . . . Jorinda Carmen Emily Credence, twenty-fourth of February. Written in pencil on the top of the page, almost as if someone *wanted* it to be easy to find, were the numbers 2402, as fresh and clear as if they had been written only yesterday. I had the codes to the gate and to the front door. Now, it seemed, I might have a third code for a third door—for the locked door at the back of the hall.

"How are you getting on?" Miss Credence's voice floated along the hall and squeezed in under the door. Quickly and quietly, I put the book on the desk, and shot back to the second bookcase just before she burst into the room. "Oh, you *have* done well, that looks so much better. It just shows what a little tender, loving care will do, doesn't it, and it would make my father so happy to see his books dusted and lined up. You know, in those days he was the only New Zealander to have articles published in *Philosophy and Literature*. Of course, there was jealousy, and he didn't have many friends among his colleagues, which made it so rewarding for him when I grew up, and could read his essays and talk them over with him, so that he felt less isolated. He was lonely, poor man, because the others just weren't up to his level . . . good enough in their way, but not in his league, really, except for Clemence, but Clem was so much younger. My father used to get a little impatient with Clem, which wasn't always fair, because Clem was bright . . ." Here her rattle of words stopped. She paused, not ending her sentence

so much as leaving it broken off, hanging and bleeding in mid-
air. Then she plunged on. "And though in the beginning he came
here to talk to my father, Clem grew very fond of me . . . " Stopping again, her mouth hanging open a little, she caught her
breath and struggled on. "But there was no future in it because
my mother died. Poor little thing, I think things had grown too
much for her *in more ways than one.*"

She made this last comment sound peculiarly significant, nodding, almost winking at me, as if I would understand what she
was getting at. "Now, how about tomorrow evening? There's
still a lot to do, but we must make haste slowly. Will you
promise to come back and finish the bookcases, wipe down the
walls, that sort of thing?" She went over to the picture of
Ginevra-Rinda and smiled into the eyes of the smiling child.
"And it was rather the same thing with Rinda. I mean, we were
always close, but in the end the world called her, and you have
to go when the world calls, so I had to give her up, but somehow,
I don't know how it is, you keep your children close by letting
them go, don't you? Oh, and you could dust all the ledges, too.
And wipe well into the corners."

Talking about what I might do tomorrow, I realized, was Miss
Credence's way of telling me to go. As I walked out, she followed
me to the door.

"You still owe me some time," she called after me as I set off
down the long drive. "Don't forget!"

The sun had set, and I walked home through a clear twilight. I
suppose I already knew what I was going to do the next day, but
was planning it in a way that was totally secret, even from me

myself, because I didn't want to admit that I was planning anything at all.

Real Life

Our house in Edwin Street changed from one thing to another as I came toward it. To begin with, it looked like a captive, struggling to escape from a cage of pipes and walkways. But then, as a row of lighted windows showed up along the side, it turned into a comic strip.

Athol was sitting on the step, reading. Well, he had a book open on his knee. He might have just brought it out there for security.

"Hello, you!" he said. I looked right, left, up and down. No one!

"Hello, you!" I murmured back to him, like a well-trained echo.

"Where's Sammy?" he asked. That really surprised me.

"I don't know," I said, shaking my head, and acting out silence even though I was talking.

"Well, I hope he turns up soon," Athol said. "Not that it's a lot of fun for him here, poor kid. I mean, you look really spooked yourself, and you're used to it."

I could have sat down beside him on the step right then and told everything . . . about the ginger cat, and that tray with the invalid feeding cup on it, and I could even have whispered that the child in the picture couldn't possibly be anyone called Rinda. I could even have confessed that I had lost the power to change into something marvelous, and that my secret story had somehow broken free, and was twisting back on me with its jaws open.

But instead of telling, I merely asked a question.

"What are you doing out here?"

"Too much noise in *there*," he said, jerking his thumb back at our front door. "Mike actually lost his temper with all of us, with Annie, too. And Sap's slammed off to her room to sulk because everyone has been ordering her to shut up. And Ginevra's worrying about Sammy, but at the same time she's telling anyone else who worries that he can look after himself, which is probably true. And now you turn up with your hair standing on end. Have *you* done something to Sammy? Struck him down and buried the body at Squintum's House?"

"I haven't seen him," I said.

I felt the words flying out between my lips as if they couldn't wait to be free. Once spoken, they were gone, and part of me was gone with them. So I shut my mouth quickly, in case other words flew after them and bled all my magic out of me, leaving me dull and ordinary. I ran up the steps past Athol, not going into the house, but climbing the Brett ladder onto the walkway. Athol watched me, smiling.

"Don't step backward too suddenly," he said. And then he seemed to make up his mind about something, leapt to his feet, and darted inside, carrying his book with him.

The planks felt thick and secure underfoot, but I wanted to go unseen. I dropped to my hands and knees and crawled carefully to the place where Sap and I had crouched on Saturday, and, just as it had then, a voice, Mike's, floated up to me.

"People can be just as sickly over difficulties as happiness," he was saying, and I knew he was talking to Annie. "Don't let's get bogged down by a lot of sentimental wallowing in trouble . . . not that we haven't got a few troubles, but I don't think we're doing too badly."

"Well, I know life doesn't care if we're happy or not, just as long as we keep on—you know—keeping on," Annie chimed in, agreeing with him. "But . . ."

"Right!" said Mike, cutting her off. "So don't be a goat! No 'butting.'"

"Why does everyone act as if I think I'm perfect and have to be cut down to size?" Annie cried.

"Because you're *there!*" said Mike, and laughed.

Their low voices rose like smoke from under the glass of the open skylights.

I crawled on to the next lighted window . . . the next picture in the Rapper comic strip.

"I do want to tell," Ginevra was saying, "but I don't want everyone to think I'm slinking home beaten. I don't want to *apologize.*"

"Don't, then!" said Athol. They must have just started this conversation, because only a few minutes ago Athol had been out on the steps, yet it sounded as if they'd been at it for hours. Perhaps they'd picked up on something they'd been talking about on and off all day.

"It's easy for you. You live in fairyland," Ginevra said scornfully.

"Well, pardon my gauzy wings!" cried Athol. "I admit I wouldn't get any sort of buzz from smashing cars, if that's what the real world means to you, but I'm not altogether off the planet. I think that if you tell Annie, she'll burst out apologizing for God knows what, and then fall all over you—as well as she can without adding to your bruises."

I crawled on gently, to the third window on that side of the house. It was completely silent, but, funnily enough, this was the only room where I could see anything much. I looked down through a gap, and in a narrow slot of space I saw Sap lying on her bed. She gave me a fright at first for she was twitching and wiggling like Frankenstein's monster with electricity running through him. But *then* I saw she was listening to some band on a Walkman, and doing a sort of horizontal dance to the beat. I even thought I could make out the influence of Sammy.

I watched for a minute, then crawled to the next right-angled turn of the walkway, and the window to the study, which was dark. But I didn't turn with the walkway. Instead, I stood up, and leaned on the scaffolding to watch lights coming on all over the south, and to stare at the lighted columns of the city center.

There I was, up above everyone else once more, looking down on the world, and suddenly I felt myself beginning to turn into something else. I didn't know what. It was too soon to say just who it was that was being born up there. But I could feel that new person, a person who was real *and* true, struggling up out of the husk of Jorinda, the bird girl, who had struggled, in turn, out of the unnamed child of the trees.

Five minutes later I walked back around the house, no longer worrying if anyone could hear me trampling over their heads. As I went, I glanced sideways to glimpse Sap alone in her room, then saw Ginevra, just for a flash, as she said, "I really enjoyed the Stock Car Circus, even though it was lonely most of the time." Somewhere below the next window Annie suddenly exclaimed, "But it gets so *lonely*."

I wondered if this was how the Bretts saw us . . . a comic strip, flashing up in window after window, words floating out in speech balloons, clustered together like any family, but lonely, too.

And there was Sammy, out in the dusk, staring up at me as if I were a ghost. He stood at the bottom of the steps, looking shut out and much lonelier than anyone inside the house could possibly be. But perhaps I looked just as solitary to him, standing above the warm light that spilled from the window across the veranda, half dissolved into the darkness, my silence surrounding me like a zone that no one else could enter.

— PART FOUR —

Real Life

Breakfast again. Sooner or later, it's always breakfast. We're warned against skimping it. It's supposed to settle us down so that we don't feel too light-hearted and drift off into the day like balloons.

Sammy was sprawling in my blue chair once again, elbows sticking out, feet, huge in their laced-up running shoes, side by side in front of him. I think if there had been a chair near the doorway that's where he would have wanted to be. Outside, overhead, feet shuffled slowly and carefully past us. Colin's voice called, "OK! I'll take the strain."

"Eat your cornflakes. Waste not! Want not!" said Mike in the kitchen.

"Want not! Waist not!" replied Sap, putting her hands to her own waist, and wiggling her hips. "I need to diet."

"I thought you were too liberated to care about things like that," said Athol, walking past, weighed down on one side by his book. He paused when he saw that I was already sitting at the table . . . only for a moment, but enough to show me that he was used to having the whole table to himself. But this breakfast was like the Mad Hatter's tea party with everyone having to move one place farther on in order to make room for Sammy.

And then a sling, with Ginevra's plastered-up arm in it, came into the room, with Ginevra right behind it. She didn't bother to say good morning, or to look at anyone except Annie.

"Annie," she said, marching up to stand eye to eye with Annie. "Listen. I shall say this only once. Are you truly listening?"

Athol stopped in the very act of opening his book. Sap stopped. Mike stepped into the kitchen doorway. I didn't check on Sammy (because I had turned toward Ginevra too), but I expect he was probably watching her as well. As for Annie, she forgot everything else in the world. All she wanted to do was to listen to what Ginevra had to say.

"Remember I told you I was able to look after myself?" Ginevra asked. "Well, I can, but I do need help—just a trace of it. I mean I've got enough money to make a down payment on a house, and that's what I'm going to do, because I don't want to go back onto the circuit even after my arm has mended. I know I told you how great it all was, but—well—I was getting sick of it. And, anyhow, even if I wanted to crash cars for the rest of my life I can't. I'm pregnant."

Behind her, I saw Mike clasp his own head as if it had begun to split open and suddenly he had to hold it together. He looked scared out of his wits. I don't suppose the silence grew any more silent, but it suddenly seemed to be jam-packed with all the things that people might be about to say. Everyone's eyes moved from Ginevra to Annie.

"Well, that's cozy," Annie said, "because I'm pregnant, too."

"You!" yelled Ginevra. "At *your* age!"

"I'm forty-six," said Annie. "It's obviously possible."

"But you're too old. It's too dangerous," cried Ginevra.

Annie laughed.

"You should talk!" she exclaimed. "What was it? *Car to topless in ten seconds?* We've all got our own ways of living dangerously."

Ginevra fell silent for a moment, frowning at Annie.

"*How* pregnant?" she asked at last.

"A bit over three months," Annie replied.

"Aha! I'm four. I'm ahead of you at last," said Ginevra, and then she burst out laughing. Though she was the one who should have been guilty, it was Annie who looked uncertain, smiling weakly.

"I made a mathematical error. I was caught out," Ginevra went on. "Not that I'm the least bit sorry . . . not by now. And, by the way, I really loved Sammy's father, even though . . . but I don't want to talk about that. Some other time!"

"Oh, Ginny," said Annie. "I don't know what to say . . ."

"Just tell me you're happy for me," cried Ginevra. "Tell me the baby's welcome. Tell me you'll *baby-sit*." And she flung her good arm round Annie. It was quite different from their first hug, at that first breakfast four days ago, because this time they seemed to collapse toward one another, even though Annie was trying not to lean on Ginevra's broken arm.

"I'm going to be an aunt!" exclaimed Sap. I saw her look down at herself. "A child aunt," she added, sounding pleased with the idea.

"Did you get caught out, too?" Ginevra asked.

Annie jerked her thumb accusingly back over her shoulder at Mike.

"We all know it was *his* fault," said Athol. "We've worked that out."

"I *wanted* this baby," Mike cried defensively. "I mean, once I knew it was on the way, I wanted it."

"You must love suffering," said Athol.

Then smoke, along with the smell of burning toast, drifted out from the kitchen, over Mike's head. A piece of crusty bread had jammed in the toaster, and had stopped it popping up in the way it was supposed to. Sap began to dance around Ginevra.

"You'll be a *single parent*," she cried. "You'll be caught in the poverty trap."

"I won't," said Ginevra crossly. "I'll be fine once I sort myself out. But my arm has to mend before I can really begin the sorting."

"Oh God, crashing cars!" exclaimed Annie suddenly. "Are you sure the baby's all right?"

"They say it's probably fine," said Ginevra. "No one ever knows for sure, do they? But any baby of mine is bound to be as tough as old boots."

"It makes me Sammy's aunt," said Sap. "Well, sort of! Are aunts allowed to marry nephews?"

She looked admiringly at Sammy, who quickly looked in the opposite direction.

Then the phone rang.

"Oh, hell," said Annie. "That'll be Carrington."

"Does *he* know you're pregnant?" cried Sap. "I bet he'll be mad with jealousy."

But it wasn't Carrington.

"It's for you," said Annie, holding out the phone to me. "Why don't you snap out with an answer, and really make my day?"

"This should be worth not hearing," muttered Athol.

"Are you there? Are you there?" asked Miss Credence, at the other end of the line. She asked it several times. "I know you won't talk back to me," she went on at last, speaking in her dry, garden voice. "I merely want to remind you that you *have* been paid in advance."

My family could see me nodding away, but the room was so crowded with the astonishment of other people's stories that nobody felt too curious about mine. And no one could tell that, though I was there at the heart of the family, I was also caught in the strange webs that blew and billowed invisibly around Squintum's House.

True Life

I worked at school with everything (the simultaneous babies, Miss Credence, Ginevra's photograph, the painted picture, the birthday book, and the codes) dancing around and changing places inside me.

When you don't talk, people often think you can't hear. I stayed in during break, and went on with my part of a drawing we were all working on . . . a long frieze that was supposed to show our togetherness and cooperation, which in a way it did, though some of us would have preferred to take our own drawings back to our own corners, to finish them there. That might have been why I decided to work on my piece after the other artists had given up and gone out to play a sort of special Kotoku House cricket in which no one suffers the humiliation of losing.

While I sat there Bruce, the therapist, drove up, and he and Coralie stood just outside the classroom door, talking in low voices, and looking in at me every few minutes. Bruce asked Coralie if there had been any change. I could tell from his resigned voice that he didn't expect any good news.

"No," I heard Coralie say. She sounded resigned, too. "Not a squeak. We don't really expect it by now. She's completely locked in. But her internal voice is perfectly intact. Take a look at this written work!"

Coralie called it an internal voice, and somewhere inside me there *was* a voice talking all the time, telling me my own story, making suggestions and casting spells, perhaps even the spell of silence. It was this voice that had ordered me to climb over the wall and explore the forest around Squintum's House. It was this voice that had commanded me to find the code that would open the door at the end of the hall. And now it was telling me that it wasn't enough just to *be* something magical. I must *do* something magical. I must push the story on, and then I really could close the book and leave it behind me. I must solve the mystery.

So, after school I went home, dumped my bike and satchel and then set off for Credence Crescent at a time when I knew Miss Credence would be at work. The iron gates seemed to sidle toward me, even though I was the one who was actually in motion. I tapped in the code, faithful old 0809, and walked, yet again, down the long drive between the lindens. My reflection showed briefly in puddles, shrunken now to hand size as I walked by. A muddy ghost with smudgy features was walking with me every step of the way, sole to sole with me. Soul to soul with me! I reached the front door, tapped in the code, 1108, heard the soft click, pushed it open, and stepped into the hall where I stood under the dusty animal heads. I remembered the feeling I had had as a little kid, looking at heads like these, that the rest of the animal was hidden in the walls of the house.

I had no permission to open doors in Squintum's House. No matter how well I knew Miss Credence, no matter how often she had reminded me that I should finish cleaning out her study, I knew that I was doing something forbidden. In fairy stories the girl who goes into the forbidden chamber will meet a terrible doom. All the same, I walked to the closed door, there at the end of the hall, and tapped in the code I had worked out the afternoon before, 2402, listening for any click there might happen to be.

Something groaned at me. Well, it began as a sigh, but turned into a groan. You read of people dying of fright, and it is almost true. Fright like that *is* a sort of death. So the world died or I died, and then, whichever one of us it was, was instantly resurrected, shaking with fear, but complete. And along with the groan, I now realized, I had heard the click I had been listening for. I pushed the door, and it opened.

I wanted to turn and run home, but I couldn't. I was compelled to go on. And the strange thing is, I felt as if I were doing something that ought to be done. Stop here, I thought, stop now! No one will ever know. But then I imagined the animals' heads, staring with their glassy eyes at the front door, all gasping in wonder at my daring. *Go on! Set us free. Break the spell*, they were saying. *Go on!*

So I went on, with the story dissolving and changing around me. I had found the forbidden key, and now I was about to enter Bluebeard's chamber.

I had guessed already that there must be a stair behind the door, and there it was, covered in dark carpet and leading upward. It bent at right angles to itself, and dim light oozed down through a skylight over the stairwell, darkened with drifts of rotting leaves. Pictures stepped up the walls, keeping pace with the stair . . . landscapes, and bowls of fruit beside dead pheasants and so on, all of them in heavy gold-colored frames. I wasn't interested in any of those pictures. I just wanted my adventure to be over and done with. All the same, on I went, up, up, up the stairs, to the landing, which gave on to a passage and doors, through one of which I glimpsed a bedroom with an unmade bed. The stairs didn't stop. They narrowed and marched on. I was climbing into the tower, climbing to the last room in Squintum's House, to the last possible door, which turned out to be firmly closed with an old-fashioned bolt. I stood outside that door, trembling and thinking, Run home! Run home now! Real life, not true! But it just wasn't possible. Once begun, the story had to be fulfilled.

So I shot back the bolt and turned the handle. The door opened easily. I stepped into the tower room, a tiny, round room, almost a dollhouse room, with a strange, pearly light flooding through the window and across the white wooden window seat. There was only one piece of furniture—a single bed. A single bed with someone sitting on the edge of it. I looked across the room into blue eyes, and knew immediately that I was looking into the eyes of the true Jorinda.

Real Life

She was wearing a dirty nightdress and a necklace of silver links. Although we were staring straight at one another, she seemed to be looking right through me, as if I weren't really there. But she must have seen me in some way, because she opened her mouth and shrieked at me. I had heard that shrieking before. I had first heard it as I stood on the edge of the ruined lawn, beating in at my ears, then fading before I could be sure I'd really heard anything. But from here, inside Squintum's House, it was fresh and raw, sound without meaning.

As soon as I actually saw Rinda I wondered why I had not known all along that it was she who was up there, waiting for me like a terrible kind of twin. But in the beginning I had thought of her as someone who had broken out of Squintum's House, and Benallan, too, and run off into the world, just as Ginevra had done. And then, once I had seen the picture, it had seemed there was no real girl—only a fairy-tale name and a face stolen from a newspaper photograph. The person I had half expected to find up there, in a horror-story way, was Conrad Hilary Credence, kept alive by forcible feeding from the invalid cup, but withered like an old coat, with his medals and glories displayed around him.

There was nothing pretty about Rinda. She hadn't become a nightingale like Jorinda in the story, and she wasn't any kind of Rapunzel. No rescuing prince could ever have climbed her thin, brown, straggling hair. She had Miss Credence's round blue eyes, without the slight squint. And even though, according to the birthday book, she must have been about eighteen, she didn't look much older than I was. We stared at each other, but I felt myself looking dismayed, whereas her gaze slid over me as if I didn't exist.

The light was pearly because it had to force its way through the white paint on the inside of the window. Not even birds were allowed to spy in on Rinda, sitting on the edge of her bed. Bars, also painted white, ran from the top to the bottom of the window frame. If she had been able to look out between the bars and through the glass, she would have seen the tops of trees, shifting and scribbling against the sky, but Rinda couldn't look out. All she could see was whiteness . . . a complete blankness. There were no pictures on the wall; there were no bookshelves. There was nothing to look at, nothing at all.

The room reeked with the sort of smell that hits you in neglected public toilets at beaches. Rinda moved, and when she moved, she clinked, for what I had taken to be a silver necklace was a chain. She was chained to that bed. She might have been able to stretch out on it, but she couldn't have moved away from it without dragging it after her. I'm not sure that she could even stand up properly. Anyhow, I knew at once that she hadn't been chained up that morning, or the day before or even the week before that. Because of the way she stooped forward like an old woman, I knew that Rinda had been held like this for so long she had taken on the pattern of her chaining.

"Jorinda!" I said aloud, giving her her full name, but she did not even glance at me.

There was a sound behind me, a quick, light, running sound growing louder and louder. I spun round as Miss Credence sud-

131

denly appeared, leaping up the last few stairs and filling the doorway.

"There you are!" she exclaimed. We stared at each other. I don't know if I looked as frightened as she did. I'm sure I must have. Then she quickly stepped down one step and slammed the door. I heard the bolt shooting across, and there I was: shut in! It had all happened in a second or two. I was locked behind the white eye of the blind tower, locked in with Rinda . . . two birds in a cage.

Real/True

I wasn't just locked in the tower. I was locked in what I had once thought of as true life. First I had flown through the tree-tops, and then I had swooped down into the garden. I had worked my way through the garden into the house, and through the house to the stair. Then I had climbed the stair to the room at the top of the tower, slipping from one story to another, from true to real and back again, and now I was locked in.

"What'll I do?" I said aloud, but I knew already that Rinda had nothing to say—to me or to anyone. She was locked into a blank room, inside as well as out.

There was a click and something like a wheeze, and suddenly I heard Miss Credence's voice, right beside my ear.

"That part of the house is strictly off-limits. It's private. You must have *known* that. What on earth am I going to do with you now?" And, for the first time, I understood something that I should have understood ages ago. Of course! There was an intercom system in Squintum's House. The gobbling sound, the groaning I had heard, were noises made by Rinda, chained in her tower room.

There was a waiting silence.

"I know you could talk if you wanted to," the disembodied voice said, at last. "What am I to do? If I let you go, you'll *tell*. And then people will come into my house, asking about Rinda. Well, as it happens I think she deserves to have her privacy respected."

There was more silence.

"I have to *protect* her," Miss Credence went on. "I'm all she has." I could tell she was waiting for me to break my rule, to plead or promise or something, but I stayed silent. At last, there was a click, and the talking air somehow closed on itself.

I had been so clever in some ways, but so dumb in others. I mean, I had noticed the codes in the birthday book, but I hadn't understood what the little grilles by the front door and by the door to the stair were, though it had been so obvious. Room could speak to room. And now I could see the blankness of the wall by the tower door was broken, not only by the door, but by a white plastic box with a little grille on top of it, and a row of buttons below it.

Though I had only been in the tower for a few minutes, it felt as if I had been there forever. And immediately a whole mass of future time, the sort of time which you know you are going to have to live through, whether you want to or not, came pressing down on me like a huge weight. My back slid down the wall; I drew up my knees. I sat on the floor, and stared over at Rinda.

Things were confused at home, but I knew I would be quickly

missed, just as Sammy had been missed yesterday evening. Mike would start saying, "Where's Hero?" Then, as soon as it grew dark, the family would look for me. Someone would come through the forest, staring up at the house, searching under the trees. And in due course, they'd even search the house, particularly if anyone caught on to Miss Credence's deep strangeness. All I had to do was wait patiently, and I would be found and set free. I knew all this, yet what I *believed* was that I would be shut inside Squintum's House for the rest of my days.

There was a click. Miss Credence was on-line again, but this time her voice was distant. It came and went because she wasn't speaking directly into the grille, but was pacing backward and forward through her dining room, gabbling—gabbling all the time, retelling an old story. And although she must have intended to talk to me, because, after all, she had turned on the intercom again, she was really talking to herself, sliding from comma to comma, full stops occurring only when she needed to take a particularly deep breath.

"It was just impossible, well, you can see that for yourself, goodness, my poor father was so upset when he knew I was expecting her, and the funny thing was, he blamed me, as if it was *my* fault, as if I'd corrupted Clem, his friend, well, his only friend by then, the only one, apart from me, who could follow his ideas. But it was just as much Clem's fault as mine, though not a fault really, because we loved one another so much, at least, he *said* he loved me, and I loved him too, because, although I was so close to my father, I missed my mother much more than I'd thought I would. Once she was gone, the whole house began to fall apart, so much dust, you know, and dishes piling up, and weeds in the garden and people who had been friends not calling anymore. But, at the time I was expecting Rinda, he was ill, my father, I mean, and he needed someone to look after him, and to feed the birds for him, and, as it turned out, his illness helped, well, what I mean is it crowded everything else out of his mind, and the drugs probably had an effect, too. There was the doctor, of course. He came and went, but he didn't seem to notice, at least he never said anything. Mind you, I'd always worn flowing clothes, and I really wasn't very big, not like some women are. And then my father died. And three months later I had her up here, all on my own. There's nothing much to that, after all, childbirth is completely natural isn't it, though I could tell almost at once—I felt certain—that there was something wrong with her, and, though I'd never wanted her I accepted the responsibility. I knew I would have to protect her for the rest of her life. And I have protected her. I've had to be cruel to be kind."

None of this was as clear as I've made it sound. Miss Credence's voice rushed into the tower room like a tide, then drew back again, fading into a mumble. Sometimes the intercom seemed to swallow the words. The sense melted away into a breathy roar. Not only this, she kept reminding herself of other things . . . her father's cleverness, the way people admired him, the reputation he had built up which could not be . . . which did not deserve to be . . . ruined by his daughter and certainly not by a faulty grandchild. I was suddenly sure that she had said all this before—that she had said it over and over again, night after night, wandering through the rooms of Squintum's House, telling herself her own story. Once she came back home from the post shop, pressed in the code and opened the door, she would meet the eyes of the mounted heads on the wall, and her true life would rush to swallow her. On the other side of the gate, in Benallan, she kept up an appearance which nobody had ever bothered to question, but out in her garden, she turned herself into her father's ghost by wearing his cloak and smoking the same kind of cigarettes that he had smoked. As she walked along the overgrown paths, some part of her watched the black, drifting figure she made, thinking, There he goes! There he goes! Still keeping guard. The dry, garden voice was probably a copy of his, too. And I understood something else (not that I quite knew I was understanding it at the time). I understood that, though she held the world at bay, she had longed (longed for many years) for a listener. Now, at last, she had one. She had me.

Rinda-Jorinda made a sound, not trying to tell me anything, just an accidental noise. And then we sat there, both silent, but with a huge difference in our silences. I had chosen mine. Rinda had never been able to choose.

It sounds calm, two silent people in a white circle, but it wasn't calm. I knew they would find me, sooner or later, but what would be left of me by then? For Miss Credence had been made strange by sadness and loneliness, and, perhaps, by being not so much a real person as a distraction on the edge of her father's life. Deep down I had always known that Miss Credence was mad. But then, what about me, for that matter? What sort of person stops talking? Real people all talk. Perhaps the silence that had made a special person of me in my talking, arguing family really showed that I was a little mad, as well.

Real Life

Then I heard footsteps on the stairs. I leapt to my feet and crouched, facing the door. It opened. Miss Credence's narrow shape filled the doorway. I didn't hesitate. I became ferocious, charging at her with teeth bared, fists flying and feet kicking. She was taken by surprise—bowled over backward. But she fell so easily that I was taken by surprise, too, and we crashed together down the stairs—bang, bang, bang—tumbling toward the first landing.

I had the advantage; I landed on top of her and I could almost have escaped, but right at the bottom of the stair, my head cracked really hard against the post at the corner of the stair. I can remember the strange, hollow sound it made, and the way everything was immediately blotted out by a flare of hard light. I had to struggle to keep any sort of hold on the world. My legs and arms were waving around but felt as if they were barely connected to me. There was no strength in them. Miss Credence rolled from under me and grabbed my arms.

"You'll be sorry! You'll be sorry!" she was screaming at me, her face only an inch or two from mine. But though it seemed to fill the world, that face was distant, too. I fought back, but it is hard to fight someone in another dimension. One of my ears, the one on the side of my head that had smacked the post, was on fire. I even thought I could see smoke drifting past my eyes.

Miss Credence was strong when she wanted to be, and right then, I was weak. We struggled, she pushing and me being pushed, step by step, up the stairs, with Miss Credence screaming into my face, and my own mouth stretched wide but making no sound.

As we reached the door, I stopped trying to grapple with her and grabbed the door frame instead. For a second or two we swayed backward and forward. But then she kicked me in the stomach, and I shot backward, falling on the floor, bent over on myself as if I were treasuring my pain. The door slammed, and I heard the bolt shoot home again.

The tower room echoed with a whooping sound. It was me, trying to fill my lungs with air. I writhed around for what felt like ages. Then, still whooping a little, I turned over and looked toward Rinda.

She seemed to be having a fit, her mouth strained wide, her fingers, crooked into claws, gouging at her own cheeks. Her eyes were dry, but her nose was running as if she were full of tears which had to force their way out of her in any way they could. But, as I whooped and watched, she stopped raking at herself, and began rubbing this watery snot into her skin and hair.

She did this in utter silence. That was the unearthly thing . . . her fury and fear made no sound at all. As I lay on the floor I watched her trying to scratch herself out of existence, knowing that she was screaming in the only way she was allowed to. It suddenly occurred to me that, even though the Credence house had no close neighbors, the sound of a crying baby might have made itself heard—in the children's playground, for instance. Somehow, Miss Credence had taught Rinda lessons of silence. I knew she *could* scream, but she never did when there was anyone in the room with her. So she *could* be taught. She *could* learn.

As I watched, the fury or fear, or whatever it was, died out of her, and she began to stare ahead of her in what seemed to be her usual manner, her cheeks striped scarlet by her own scraping fingers.

"I trusted you," said Miss Credence, her voice coming over the intercom, like a ghost through a keyhole. "Why have you done this to me? You were like my true daughter to me. I *liked* you."

I had nothing to say, but she persisted.

"Tell me!" she commanded. "I know you can talk, so go on . . . tell me, because you'll have to talk sooner or later. We'll be spending a lot of time together."

But I would not answer her.

Then she began to wander around, talking to herself once more, so that her voice swelled and faded, swelled and faded.

"Don't you see, I've had to *protect* Rinda . . . look after her carefully . . . because she can't choose for herself." The voice mumbled on, an inner voice becoming an outside one. "Perhaps it was pride, but why should one suffer for liking oneself, one's own talents? I mean, let's face it, no false modesty, I was a clever girl, well, I *am* clever, I'm in the top two and a half percent, there's no doubt about that, because I was tested, and I became a member of MENSA. I could have flown. My father . . . well, of course he was proud of me, but he knew that the world is hard on clever women, and I think, when he pulled me back, that he might have been trying to protect me, though it may have been partly self-interest, too, because there was no one else, you know . . . no one to be a real companion to him, apart from Clem for a while. And those days were lovely days, but then Clem went off to Auckland with his wife and children, his wife was nothing much (a very *ordinary* mind), and I never saw him again, though I still get a card every Christmas, from California last time, so you see he's done very well." Her voice mumbled away into nothing; I think she must have gone into the kitchen.

I don't know how much time went by, but I know it did go by. On the other side of the white window, dusk began to fill the Credence forest. I began to imagine darkness gathering under the trees, the blue fading to gray, and the gray deepening to black. Stars would be coming out . . . Orion riding high, Sirius the dog star, and Canopus, all looking down on the tower . . . and street-lights would begin shining down on Credence Crescent and Edwin Street.

"Everything I've done for Rinda I've done for her own good," Miss Credence said, suddenly coming back on-line again, and still making excuses. "My father used to talk about the survival of the fittest, which was all very well for him, what with him being so sure he *was* one of the fittest. And, fit or not, he was always *looked after*, because (I will say this for my mother) she did look after him, and so did I. Nobody could say I didn't rally when my turn came."

Suddenly a phone rang. I could hear it quite clearly, though of course it was ringing downstairs.

"Yes," said Miss Credence. Then I heard her say, "Dear me, how worrying for you. No, I haven't seen her. Actually, I was expecting her this evening, but . . . no sight or sound. Well, there wouldn't be any sound, would there?" Her voice stopped. I think she must have been listening. "I do hope she's all right," she said at last, "though the streets seem so unreliable these days, not safe in the way they used to be. Not that I mean to worry you, but we do hear such horror stories. Still, Jorinda's a sensible girl. Hero, I mean. Jorinda's my pet name for her. She wouldn't go off with any stranger. I'll tell you what! I'll go out with a flashlight and give her a call, just in case . . . No! No trouble at all. Let me know immediately there's any news."

I suddenly thought of shouting through the intercom. Whoever was ringing and asking about me might hear me in the background if I yelled "Help! Help!" loudly enough. But, as I made for the grille, I heard her ring off.

"You see?" she said from the room downstairs. "You're causing such worry to so many people. And I can't even come up and feed Rinda in case you attack me again. All this is making me miserable." Then she clicked off, and was gone.

There's no real point in telling about the next hours. Shivering and aching from the fight, I lay on the floor. I didn't dare to share Rinda's bed. And I didn't *want* to. It seems awful, but I couldn't bear the thought of touching her in any way. We lay there, Rinda and I, sharing the same space, but in our different places and different silences.

In the end I actually went to sleep. I was worn out, but it wasn't just that. Somehow I shrank away from the world, from the hard floor and the cold (for I was cold, even on a summer night). And in due course my private silence within the silence of the room turned into the sort of miserable sleep that comes and goes. I dreamed of voices calling my name, and chains rattling as Rinda shifted in her bed, but I did sleep.

Suddenly, I woke to hear a terrible shriek and a crashing sound. I sat up, drew up my knees and flung my arms around them, alarmed to find myself crying in the dark. There was another shriek. I thought, I *hoped*, that the police or someone else might have broken in. Any minute now the door might burst open and I might be rescued. I ran to the intercom and yelled, "Help! Help!", weeping as I yelled, stretched until I thought I would tear in two, pulled in different directions by hopes and fears. The screaming went on and on, and not only screaming but crashing, too. Glass shattered. Something splintered. On and on! On and on! When you haven't got any choice you can get used to something like that. By the time it stopped, I had almost stopped caring.

And it did stop, at last. Everything grew quiet again except for the wind, which rubbed itself against the white window, purring like the ghost of a cat.

Real/True

When I woke again I could hear blackbirds singing. They sounded like voices struggling through from another world on the edge of this one. I turned my head toward the blank window, and knew at once that, out there, the treetops would be drenched in light. Day was working its way through the opaque whiteness, and I was bathed in that pearly glow. And, in spite of my restless night on the floor, I found I was feeling suddenly alert, more capable, more *alive*, than I had felt since the first shock of finding myself locked in with Rinda. Perhaps that fight on the stair had left me stunned. I still felt I was in a story, but it was *my* story once more. I didn't have to sit there, waiting to be rescued. I could alter the end . . . break the window . . . climb out onto the roof. Perhaps I would have thought of doing this before, if there had been anything in the room that could have been used to break glass. Yet now I remembered seeing an episode of *Pharazyn Towers* in which Delpha, the girl reporter for *Songline*, a city magazine, was abducted and locked on the upper floor of a deserted warehouse. But she had simply wrapped her stylish jacket around her hand, and had smashed the windows easily.

I turned over onto my stomach and shot a look at Rinda, who was nothing but a long shape in her bed. And then I saw a chamber pot under her bed. I realized, with surprise, that I had stopped noticing the smell of the room which had seemed so dreadful when I first stepped into it. The sight of that pot immediately made me want to pee. I stood up and began jiggling around the room, partly to distract myself, even though I knew I'd have to go sooner or later, and partly to keep my new, lively thoughts on the move. In the beginning it was a poor, limping jiggle because I was bruised and stiff, but I did loosen up, tucking my hands into my own armpits as I jiggled, trying to squeeze warmth back into myself. And as I limped and squeezed and my blood began moving more freely, I began thinking what a wimp I'd been, just flopping down, giving in to fear. I made excuses for myself. Perhaps it had been shock. But now . . . now there must be something a hero would do . . . *could* do. First of all, I jiggled over to the window and tugged experimentally at the white bars. The very first one I tugged at just came away in my hand. I had imagined they must be steel, because bars are supposed to be made of steel. But not these bars! I was holding a simple rod of wood. The bars weren't welded—just nailed, and not very soundly. I had been looking at the *idea* of a cage, rather than a real one. And, now I looked closely, I could see the pale inner surface, painted onto the glass, was crackling all over. Fine lines ran through and through the white paint. I picked, experimentally, at the white paint with my thumbnail.

The paint easily gave up its hold on the glass and flaked away in a little snowstorm. Within a minute I had made a peephole about as big as a twenty-cent piece, and was able, by pressing my eye right against the glass, to look out into the garden. You know what it's like; when you put your eye close to a hole, even a pinhole, you can see a surprising amount. There was a small circle of morning. There were the treetops. A blackbird, poised on top of a linden, was singing and singing, guarding his second nest of the season. And then, as I squinnied out, there in the middle distance a branch swept down across my view, and I thought that I was going to see my own ghost on one of those leafy highroads I knew so well. But the feet that came edging into my circle of sight wore huge laced-up running shoes.

During the night I had dreamed of my family searching for me, all calling my name over and over again, even though, in my dream, I couldn't answer. Sammy had not been one of the searchers, and yet it was definitely Sammy who was out there now. I suddenly understood that Sammy, with nothing to do and no place of his own, had entertained himself by tracking me on my journeys to Squintum's House, that he had seen me climb the wall and lose myself in the trees.

I didn't hesitate. Almost as if I'd already dreamed what I must do, I ran to the bed, scrabbled under it for the chamber pot (holding my breath as the stink hit me), sloshed what was in it all over the floor, ran back to the window, and then thumped the window with the pot. I thought the glass would break as easily as it had broken in *Pharazyn Towers*, but the pot just bounced back at me, hitting me square on the nose. It really hurt, but I swung again, furiously this time, shutting my eyes as I struck.

The glass shattered. Little slivers flew toward me like transparent gnats, nipping my forehead and cheeks, and within a second I heard more glass splintering on the bricks below . . . bricks which I had cleaned and weeded only the week before. Fresh air burst in on me. The pot leapt out of my hand, and a second later I heard it crash below.

I opened my eyes. There, on the other side of a jagged star, across a chasm of morning light, was Sammy, staring back at me from among the nearest branches. I wished I had a great braid of hair, thick as a rope, to throw across to him. He could have tied it to a branch in the tree, and then run across into Squintum's House on a tightrope made from a living part of me.

I didn't hesitate. I spoke out as if I had never, ever been silent.

"Get help!" I called. "She's shut me up here."

"No shit!" Sammy yelled back. "Hey, I told them you walked around in the trees. I *told* them!"

"Get Mike!" I yelled. "Get Mike! Get Mike!"

I said it at least three times, but it seemed to be all I could say.

"They've been looking everywhere. Cops, too!" he said, peering at me. "Hey, what's she *done* to you?"

I looked down and saw blood on my hands. At the same time I felt a movement like caterpillars on my upper lip. My nose was bleeding.

"Get Mike!" I cried again. "Bring something to cut chains."

"Chains?" said Sammy, incredulously. "Shit!"

But every single thing he said sounded wonderful to me.

"There's someone else in here chained to the bed," I went on, and heard steps on the stairs. "She's coming," I screamed. "Tell Mike! Go on! Get out! Now!"

"Someone else?" cried Sammy, as he scrambled back along the branch at last.

The door opened behind me. I turned, spreading myself in front of the broken window, trying, I suppose, to hide the broken star and protect Sammy, the cool cat of the forest. Miss Credence stood there wrapped in the black cloak, her black hat slanted across her head. She strolled toward me, quite gently, as if we both had plenty of time. I began screaming as she came up to me, prepared to die by forcing my way out across jagged glass.

"Just step aside, Jorinda," Miss Credence said, and now she was speaking in her first voice, that dry, half-amused, rustly garden voice that I thought might be a version of her father's. Behind her, Rinda was sitting up in bed. I could hear the clink of her chains. I didn't move, but Miss Credence looked over my shoulder, through the dangerous edges in the middle of the window, and I imagined her catching a glimpse of Sammy as he made for the wall.

"Well," she said. "A cat among the pigeons!"

"Get out!" I yelled, without turning around.

Miss Credence laughed.

"He's gone! Off and away," she said. "Friend of yours?"

I shot a glance over my shoulder, and saw nothing now but shaking leaves. When I looked back at Miss Credence she was watching me with one eye, but the other seemed to be gazing past me at the leaves and the sky beyond. She scratched her cheek thoughtfully, probably not knowing that, behind her, Rinda was gouging her own cheeks, and opening her mouth in one of those dreadful, silent screams. As I stared, Rinda sank her teeth into her own forearm, and worried her own flesh, like a dog at a bone.

"Well, that's it, then," said Miss Credence at last, still in her father's voice. She was like an entirely different person from the woman who had babbled and screamed the night before. "It's a relief, really. A relief. I woke up this morning, and I knew . . . I knew I'd gone too far. Made a mistake! You know, great intelligence can sometimes be close to . . . to something else." And she gave me a strange smile . . . a smile with which she somehow forgave herself for her own madness and violence because her particular kind of madness and violence proved she was too clever for the ordinary world.

"I don't believe intelligence is close to that other thing," I said. "I think it's the opposite."

They were the first words I had ever said to her.

"Oh, you've suddenly found a voice, have you?" she replied sharply. "Those of us in the top two and a half percent can't be judged by the same rules as ordinary people." Then she sat down in the window seat, pulled her knees up, wrapping the cloak right around herself, so that she looked like a black triangle with a head on top, and stared out through the hole in the window at the forest beyond.

"It really was a very beautiful garden when I was a child," she said in a light, reminiscing voice. "We used to have garden parties, and I would help to pass the cakes around. I thought it would always be like that . . . you know . . . the dappled light, the talking and laughing, with my father looking so artistic in his cloak (no one else ever wore a cloak), and everything running so smoothly. But then, after my mother died, people stopped calling in."

I began thinking about making a dash for the door, which stood slightly open, because this slow, reflective voice frightened me as much as the angry, babbling one. It sounded so reasonable, but I knew—I *knew*—that Miss Credence's reason, her order, was built on toppling ruins. The wrong movement on my part might set it all crumbling, and that other desperate, uncontrolled creature would come rushing out at me through the cracks. So I sat down too, slowly and carefully, at the other end of the window seat, forcing myself to be a patient listener, and all the time, from this angle, just beyond Miss Credence's right ear and through the jagged star, I could see a whole slot of Benallan, with our house, caught in its cage of pipes and walkways, in the middle of the view. There, in Squintum's House, I fixed my eyes on home. *I'll be back soon*, I vowed to myself with the inside voice of my past silence. *Soon! Soon! Soon!*

"I've been very silly," said Miss Credence in a puzzled voice. "But I was never a particularly *practical* person." Once again she sounded superior. The top two and a half percent of people were above the necessity of being practical. "I suppose I could have asked for help, but you know"—she looked into the air and then down at the floor, with a glance that somehow seemed to pierce the worn wood— "in my way I'm a haunted house. A haunted house, as well as the actual ghost that does the haunting. And as for"—here she jerked her head back toward Rinda who was now sitting almost exactly as she had been when I first saw her—"I told you I loved her (didn't I tell you that? I often hear myself saying it) but I suppose, really, I hated her. That's the truth of it. And yet . . . not quite the truth, either . . . " Her voice trailed away. She sounded puzzled, though not pathetic. She was thinking it over, and not finding the right words; she was *musing.*

The blackbirds had stopped singing. The sun was bright on the tops of the trees, though the trunks stood in deep shadow.

"It was a lovely garden once," Miss Credence began again, but not sounding too sure about it this time round, and I said, "It's a forest now."

"I could have given her away," Miss Credence continued as if I hadn't spoken. "There are institutions"—just for a moment there, she sounded a little like her downstairs, babbling self— "which would have taken her in. But it would have been like *treachery.* I mean people (a lot of *university* people, I'm sorry to say) were jealous of my father's intelligence. I could imagine them all smirking over him if we had a child in the family who wasn't quite . . . " She paused. "I thought of killing her when she was born," she added casually. "All I would have had to do was to hold a pillow over her face for a few minutes, and it would have changed everything. I could have planted her out under one of the trees and no one would ever have known. But there you are. I was sentimental. I didn't do it. Well, not very often, and never enough to kill her. Only now and then, to stop her crying. And so she lived." And she looked briefly over at Rinda. "Well, it's a sort of life, isn't it?"

The sound of traffic came faintly in through the broken window. The city was stretching and purring out there.

"You should have told Clem," I said, and, in my own ears, I sounded like Ginevra. "He should have helped you."

"Clem," Miss Credence replied. "Clem! Oh dear, if I'd breathed a word to Clem, I don't think I'd ever have received so much as a Christmas card."

She went on staring, still musing, I suppose, drawing threads of the past through her memory, untangling them from one another and setting them in order.

"They're going to close the Benallan branch . . . *my* branch," she said at last, watching the treetops ripple a little in the breeze. "My post office. It's not just a *shop*, no matter what the government suddenly decides to call it. Anyway, that's why I came home early yesterday. To hell with it, I thought. All those years, and then suddenly an official 'Get thee gone!' So I rang up Mrs. Adams, who stands in for me sometimes, told her I was feeling ill, and walked out. And deep down I almost thought you might be here. I've been inviting you, haven't I? I mean, when I wrote those codes in pencil in the birthday book, and then asked you to clean the study, wasn't I leaving clues, *just in case*? I think I must have been. I think—I really think—I've had enough. I must have wanted it all over and done with."

"That's my sister's picture on the wall in the study," I said. "The one you told me was a painting of Jorinda."

She looked astonished.

"Your *sister*? I did think it looked a little like you."

"The photograph was in the paper ages ago," I pointed out, but she took no notice.

"I read about you . . . about *her* . . . a few years after Rinda was born, and I knew at once that was the picture of my true child, the one I *should* have had. I wrote to the newspaper office and bought a big copy of that picture (it's lying around in a drawer somewhere) but I didn't hang the photograph on the wall. That would have been cheating. I copied it, which made it mine, and hung my own copy. I think that was fair enough, don't you?" She stared at me. "Your sister!" she said in a wondering voice. "No wonder you looked so familiar when you slid from the trees and fell at my feet. I half thought you might turn into the true Rinda . . . Jorinda. After all, you can't have been very happy in your own home, or why would you have stopped talking?"

I had never quite answered this question, even to myself . . . well, not properly. I only knew that my silence was the way in which I had made myself special, made myself powerful in a family in which everyone struggled to find their own power.

"Not talking's my way of being famous," I said, knowing, for the first time, that this was true. In a family that let words flow away like wasting water, silence had been an alternative authority. I couldn't be Ginevra, because she was already ahead of me, so I had become her opposite, instead. I remembered what Athol had said of Ginevra. It was true of me, too. "I wanted to be a magician," I said aloud.

Out of the distant purr of airport traffic, the voice of one particular car made itself heard. Miss Credence turned her head, listening. It stopped, and I think we both relaxed a little in the pearly light of the tower room. But after a short silence, the engine roared again—really roared. There was a distant, metallic sound, which made Squintum's forest tremble. And then that car was tearing down the drive, scraps of scarlet flashing up to us from under the linden trees. Then our Volkswagen charged across the meadow, and spun to an amazing stop outside the front door. There was a great dent in its curved front, and one headlight was smashed. A strange, padded, helmeted alien leapt from behind the driver's seat. Sammy! Ginevra struggled out from the passenger seat, cast and all, helmeted, too, with a black safety helmet, the hat of a *modern* magician. I supposed her broken arm had stopped her from driving herself, but she had had Sammy to help her. They had commandeered the nearest car, roared down Credence Crescent and had stopped at the iron gates. Ginevra would have struggled out to inspect the rusting chain that held them together, then struggled in again, belted up, and talked Sammy through the process, first of backing down Credence Crescent, and then driving our car straight into the gates, using her special, strange skills, her mathematics—her magic—to burst them open. Out from under the lindens ran Athol and Mike. We have seat belts in the back of the Volkswagen, but there would have been no helmets, no special padded suits for them to wear. Sammy began shouting, and pointing up at the window through which Miss Credence and I were staring down.

"There they are!" said Miss Credence, as if these wild strangers were friends come to a garden party. "What has happened to that poor young man? Has he broken his arm?"

"It's my sister!" I explained. "The one you painted."

And now Miss Credence frightened me all over again, just as I was growing hopeful. Miss Credence wailed.

"Jorinda?" she cried. "What have you done to her, you people out there? What have you done to that dear little girl?"

"She did it to herself," I cried back. "She *chose* it."

Miss Credence took a deep breath, and turned away from the star-shaped view of the outside world.

"Promise to stay here," she said, smiling, almost as if she were fond of me. "I'll promise not to hurt anyone if you promise to stay here until I've let them in."

"All right! I do promise," I said. Then she did something in such a way I thought she might be doing it for the first time in their entire lives together. She moved over to Rinda, who shrank as she approached. But Miss Credence gave her a quick kiss, the sort of kiss you give to a stranger out of politeness, then almost skipped to the door, paused there, and nodded at me.

"I'll let myself out," she said. I listened to her feet on the stairs and to the voices down in the garden. The click and brush of the opening door floated up the stairwell.

I swung my trembling legs up onto the window seat, and knelt there, trying to see what was happening at the front door, and, as I did this, a huge piece of glass tumbled out of the top part of the frame to crash onto the bricks below. It almost hit Sammy, who was standing back from the front door, looking up at the tower window. He saw me and shouted.

"Hey! There she is. There she *is!*"

Athol appeared beside him, cupping his hands on either side of his eyes to keep the early sunshine from reflecting in his glasses.

"Hero!" he yelled up to me. "We're on our way. We're going to smash the door in." I don't think I'd ever heard such a mixture of fear and happiness in any voice before.

"She's coming to let you in," I called.

"Hero's talking," I heard him saying to someone, and then he looked up at me and shouted, "Don't stop!"

I heard a door slam, but it wasn't the front door. There was something familiar about the sharpness of the sound . . . about the edge that seemed to cut into me. I remembered myself walking up the drive last Saturday morning and hearing the slam of that very same door.

"1108! The code is 1108," I yelled down, heard quick voices and the sound of the front door opening. And then, immediately, voices burst out of the air around me because Miss Credence had left the intercom channel between the rooms open all night, probably so that she could hear me if I tried escaping. "What's happened here?" I heard Ginevra cry. "Someone's trashed the place." And now, promise or no promise, I ran to the tower door. Promise or no promise, I stumbled down the stairs and opened the door into the hall, only to be snatched into Mike's arms. As they all milled around us—Athol, Ginevra, Sammy—I began to cry in real earnest, and they hurried me out of the crowded hall into the sitting room.

Ginevra was right. The whole place had been trashed. Everything that could be broken was broken, the mounted heads had been wrenched from the wall, pages torn from books, chairs smashed against walls. The picture frames were empty now, twisted out of shape. The fireplace was in total mourning, choked with shapeless lumps, blackened, charred and smoldering. Ghostly words shone briefly on burnt paper and then crumbled away. In the kitchen, the refrigerator door hung open over a floor that was covered with pools of milk, slices of bread, and spots that looked like drops of blood but were really patches of jam. The rings on the stove glowed red-hot through fine white ash.

"Hero! Hero, listen! Sammy says there's someone chained up in the tower," Mike cried, shaking me gently, though he looked anything but gentle.

"Yes," I cried, "but not Miss Credence. She must have run out the back door." And I had a sudden picture of her, fleeing from the house she had destroyed in the early hours of the morning, escaping her prison, springing out into her forest, her true forest, like an enchanted traveler in *Old Fairy Tales*. Once there she would keep on wandering, deeper and deeper, always surrounded by marvels, while the back door of Squintum's House cracked shut behind her.

She had gone out through the back door, and she had gone further in, but not further into her forest. Miss Credence had lifted her father's gun from its brackets, taken it through the kitchen, into a little backyard between the house and the stone wall, and had shot herself in the head. She had let herself out.

You'd think that would have been enough to kill her, but it wasn't. An ambulance took her to hospital, where they worked hard and saved her life. Not that she could do anything with what they saved. She just lay there in the hospital for the rest of her days, staring up at a white ceiling. She lay there in utter silence.

—— Part Five ——

Real Life

Coming down Edwin Street, Hero looked up and saw her own house with surprise. The story that had flowed through her for the last three years had suddenly flooded the world around her once more. But the Bretts and the scaffolding were long gone. They would be moving past other windows, looking in on other comic strips. That's why soap operas are so popular, thought Hero. Their stories are like exciting gossip, which you can listen in on without feeling guilty. She thought of her own soap opera, the story that she had printed out last night. For nearly three years she had tried to discover everything it had to tell, but last night she had printed it out. Now, it was no longer contained by the screen but sitting secretly under her bed—a pile of pages, fluttering at the top and uneven around all its edges, it seemed to be moving toward a freedom of its own.

But over the years one thing had not changed. As she approached the door, passionate voices burst in on her. Argument again! A family row! There they all were—Mike, Annie, Ginevra, Athol, and Sammy, and even the two little ones, Ginevra's Cassie and Annie's Toby, lying side by side behind the blue chair. Out in the kitchen Hero could see Sap standing beside the open fridge, drinking milk straight from the bottle.

"Why not?" Annie was crying aloud. "We can make room."

But Mike shouted even more loudly.

"No!" he exclaimed. "No! No! No!"

The little ones looked around at the angry voices, but they were too used to arguments to worry. They started giggling and pushing each other.

It seemed Mike was being relentless, for once. Hero edged into the room. Sammy raised his eyebrows at her, and pointed silently to a corner of the table. Hero saw, with amazement and something like fear, a block of pages, held together by a rubber band. Though she was quite prepared to listen, and even, these days, to take part in a good family argument, Hero suddenly lost interest in anything that Mike and Annie might have to say to each other.

"My story!" she cried. No one took any notice of her, which was a change. She had been talking for three years, and yet her voice often had the power of a stranger's.

"Room for one more," Annie was saying in an urgent, coaxing voice. "Mike, it's the *kind* thing to do. With all our faults we're a wonderful family. Especially you! Room for one more!" she said again, as if she were pronouncing a spell.

"I can't bear to be any more wonderful than I am already," said Mike. "Listen, Annie . . ."

"If we turn the study into a bedroom-study . . . " Annie interrupted him, begging, not demanding.

Hero stared past them at her story. She had planned to hide it at the back of the bookcase (behind *The Jungle Book* and *Old Fairy Tales*, perhaps) and to try to take it by surprise in a week or two. She had not imagined anyone else reading those defenseless pages until she had reread them herself, and turned them into a something both real and true, outside her own authorship.

"Did I say you could?" she cried so loudly that they had to take notice. Mike looked over at her, and then in a guilty but distracted way at the pile of pages.

"We didn't mean to," he said apologetically. "I was nosy. I found it under your bed when I was vacuuming and I couldn't help glancing over the first page. And then, once I started I just kept on and on . . . and, after all, that's what print is for, isn't it? You must have meant it to be read."

Annie looked over at the pages as well, and forgot her argument with Mike.

"I read it too," she cried. "And Hero—you're a *writer*. You really are." She said the word *writer* as if she were announcing a great victory for Hero. As she spoke, she looked at Hero with a mixed expression, amazed, delighted, and somehow scheming.

Hero struggled with feelings of betrayal shot through with astonishing pleasure. As she wavered between fury and happiness, Annie turned toward Mike once more, taking a deep breath as she did so.

"No!" he snapped.

"But you've always said that between us we could do anything we set our hearts on. And I've set my heart on this."

"I *know* what I said," yelled Mike so angrily that she stopped, blinking as if she had run into a wall. "And everything's changed since I said it. We've got Hero, Sap, the two little ones . . . even Sammy spends a lot of time round here."

"Sor-*ry!*" said Sammy.

"You're no trouble, Sam," said Mike quickly. "I don't mean that. But I have to—to think about you. Make room for you. I can't make room for Rinda Credence as well."

"*I'd* be here some of the time," cried Annie, as if that put everything right. "If Rinda were here, actually in the house, I'd

159

spend more time working at home. I'd . . . well, I'd *help*. I'd *watch* her. She's learning to speak. She uses a lot of word strings. It's fascinating." Annie began to speak in what Sap called her 'lecturing' voice. "We all need some sort of language to complete us. And, as far as we can tell, Miss Credence never spoke to Rinda. She was never completed, and now . . ."

Ginevra suddenly let out a howl.

"You want to write a *book* about her," she cried, and burst out laughing, but not as if she thought it was altogether funny.

"Why not?" Annie shouted. "It's what we should do . . . *use* what happens to us. Make it all *mean* something."

"Yes, but Annie," Mike began slowly, "what Rinda Credence needs—needs desperately—is full-time love, and . . . " He broke off and struggled with something inside himself. "Being brutally honest," he said at last, "I don't want to be bothered. I'm too loaded down."

"Does anyone love her?" asked Athol, his voice coming in from the side. "*Can* anyone love her? If we're being brutally honest, that is."

No one but Hero seemed to hear this terrible question.

"People from the Psychology Department are taking her over," Annie began. She sounded a little desperate. "There's some suggestion that Dr. and Mrs. Wylie might *foster* her, which means he and that student of his would be in control. Mike, we've earned our right to know her best. If it wasn't for Hero she'd still be chained to that bed. Oh, why not, Mikie? *I'd* be here."

"You'd be here on and off," said Mike. "But Annie, she's still incontinent at times; she needs all of someone's attention. And, as I keep saying, there's no room."

"She can have my room," said Athol, getting to his feet. "Moment of truth! I'm moving out."

"You're twaddlizing!" cried Sap incredulously, appearing in the kitchen doorway with the milk bottle in her hand. Even Cassie and Toby looked round. As they did so, Windcheater shot out from behind the blue chair, trying to get as close to the door as possible. He hated the little children.

Everyone else was staring at Athol in astonishment.

"I'm on my way," he said quickly, getting in before Annie could say a word. "It's all arranged. I'm going to share a warehouse in a shabby part of the inner city with a beautiful artist and an experimental sound-man. Aren't you pleased?"

"What about your thesis?" asked Mike. He sounded surprised and doubtful. "It's on the system here. And you're so close to finishing it that—"

"I've already finished my thesis," Athol answered, interrupting him. "I mean I'm finished *with* it. To tell you the truth, I haven't worked on it for ages. What I've done over the last two years is write television scripts."

"Television scripts!" Annie cried impatiently, flinging up her hands, then letting them flop down again. "Get one accepted first."

"I already have," said Athol. "It took a while but I've been paid for three and they've suggested I might commit myself to another half-dozen for the new series."

"New series of what?" asked Annie.

"Who have?" said Mike.

"The producers of *Pharazyn Towers*," Athol replied, closing his eyes and screwing up his face, as if he thought the whole new floor overhead might come crashing down on him at that dread name.

"*Pharazyn Towers*?" shouted Annie. "*Pharazyn-bloody-Towers*?"

"Annie, we *live* in bloody *Pharazyn Towers*, or something like it," Athol shouted back. "And we have to *use* what happens to us, don't we? Make it *mean* something? Anyhow, it forced itself on me. I just closed my eyes, lay back, and gave in."

"*Pharazyn Towers*," exclaimed Sap. Hugging the milk bottle, she gave a cry of rapture. "I'll know more about it than anyone else in my class."

Annie turned on Athol.

"See what you've done?" she said.

"Even if Athol moves out," Mike declared, "we're not giving his room to Rinda Credence."

Hero heard all this, but her book, sitting on the edge of the table, had a voice of its own that was even more insistent.

"Did you *really* like my story?" she asked, bringing them back to the true subject, and trying to make them praise it all over again.

"I swear someone will publish it," said Annie. Though her wish to have power over the slow, struggling changes of Rinda Credence was dominating her thoughts, she was distracted. "Suppose I go over it in more detail later on . . . make some suggestions. What do you think, Mike?"

"Have I won the argument?" asked Mike, refusing to commit himself.

"Yes," said Annie in a docile voice.

"Watch out, Mike!" Ginevra cried. "She's reorganizing her forces."

"If it's half-time, I think I'd like a beer," said Mike.

"You're on!" said Annie.

Hero picked up her pages and carried them upstairs. No one but Sammy watched her go.

Pinned up behind the word processor in the new workroom was a Polaroid photograph. It had been taken during a weekend a fortnight earlier when they had rented a cottage up in the mountains, and gone skiing. She and Sammy stood side by side, but toppling toward each other, hamming it up like clowns. Hero grinned, remembering. Time to move on! she thought. Now I have power over the memory of Squintum's House. I've turned it into a story. All I have to do is write *The End*.

She swung her chair in front of the screen, and, reaching across to the computer, she switched it on. It gave a small cry, flashing figures and messages as it checked its own systems, making sure all its different memories were in place. At last the screen turned blue. Hero touched first one key, and then another. The white print of her story leapt out of nowhere. Hero moved to the last line, and stared at it, thinking for a moment. And then, at last, her fingers raced away once more.

True

When I began my story I thought that, deep down, it was going to be about silence, because all stories, not just mine, rise out of silence of a kind. But now I think it has turned out to be about an entirely different sort of twist in the world, not silence but fame . . . about being a star.

Famous people become famous by somehow stealing energy from those around them. I can understand Rappie getting annoyed when people speak as if her true purpose in life is not jogging or playing bridge which she enjoys, but simply being Annie's mother-in-law. Or take Cassie! She talks well for someone just three years old, but people say, "Of course. She's got Annie for a grandmother," as if Ginevra is no part of her, or as if Cassie is nothing in herself. It makes Ginevra furious. Perhaps every time anyone is praised it means that someone else somewhere is going to be ignored.

I said a true thing to Miss Credence when I told her that I had wanted to be a magician; and when I told her that, I was also telling myself—admitting it for the first time. My silence was what the ones who studied my sort of muteness called *manipulative*, because I was trying to work the world to my advantage. I felt more interesting being silent than I had ever felt because of anything I ever had to say. I received a more urgent attention.

And it might have been partly self-defense. I think I believed that, if I didn't guard myself, I would become a sort of ghost haunting Annie's house, just as Miss Credence had become a ghost haunting her father's. Miss Credence couldn't run off and crash cars like Ginevra, or take notes of family arguments and use them in a secret soap opera like Athol, and she didn't choose silence like me. Instead she became a puppet of her father's glory, and that glory was not just the hand inside the puppet. It was a mouth as well . . . a mouth with teeth . . . which spoke for her in the beginning, but, in the end, turned on her and chewed her up. Now, though Annie has always loved being famous, she has always wanted to share the fame—to have us all living happily ever after, bathed in her own special sunshine.

But it's not that easy. Perhaps there's only just enough light and warmth to go around, and people like Annie, whether they mean to or not, are using up someone else's share. At times, just by being famous, they somehow seem to make other people less real—less true.

If things were fair, all stories would be anonymous. I don't mean that the storyteller wouldn't get *paid* for telling. But there would be no names on the covers of books, or interviews on television . . . just the story itself, climbing walls, sliding from tree to tree, and stealing secretly through the forests of the world, real, but more than real. Set free from the faults that go with its author's name. Made true! But of course things aren't fair. They never have been.

So these days I talk like everyone else—ask questions and answer them, make comments, give descriptions, tell jokes. I've almost given up on silence as my way of being magical. I might even be able to have a book published, a book that would have my name on the cover. Annie has just said so. But, as I heard her say it, I realized that a different sort of silence, even more magical than the first, was being born in me.

I'm going to finish my story now.

I have just said good-bye to my forest. Miss Credence died a few weeks ago, and Squintum's House and its forest have been sold to developers who are planning to build a whole complex of trendy town houses on Credence land. In the last day or two I have heard chain saws screaming among those old trees. The proceeds of the sale are going into a trust on behalf of Rinda because it costs a lot to look after her. She is a classic closet child (that's what they call children who are found shut up in cupboards or locked in attics, hidden away from the world for years). Deaf people aren't closet children. They connect with the world. They have a true language of their own. But, looking across her room for years and years, all Rinda saw was a white window set in white walls. Miss Credence fed her, but, even then, I think she always had her face turned a little away.

A woman called Sally Eddington has looked after Rinda for the last three years, defending her against the experts who study her. But Sally had a fall last week, and it'll be months before she is strong enough to look after Rinda again, because Rinda can be difficult. She has grown strong. She cries with a voice now, and even sheds tears. When something annoys or frightens her she wets herself. Someone will have to look after her, which is why the great argument is going on downstairs.

And other people have read my story. Annie wants to edit it and send it to a publisher. She's thrilled with me. At last I am what I ought to be . . . At last, she thinks, I am going to be my true self.

Once I used to pick up *Old Fairy Tales*, shut my eyes, put my blind finger blindly on a line, then open my eyes suddenly so that I could read whatever it was fate had to say to me. *Tell your sorrows to the old stove in the corner*, I read, because true life is timeless and the story already knew what lay ahead of me. And when the story gives you good advice, there's no way out. You just have to act upon it.

Real

Hero looked at what she had set down on the screen, but she did not print it out. Instead she picked up her thick manuscript, weighed it in her hands, then moved over to the wood stove on its square of deep blue tiles. She opened the black door with the glass panel set in it and pushed the block of pages in, turning her head away, perhaps making sure she would not be tempted to snatch them out again. Thick smoke suddenly gushed out toward her, not rising into the air at once, but pouring downward. The pages were too dense to burn easily, but as she prodded them with the poker, coughing and fanning the smoke away from her face with her left hand, they began to smolder at the edges. She separated them from one another as well as she could. A few caught fire; others followed. By the time she closed the door of the woodburner, her story was roaring like a lion in the long throat of the stove pipe.

So Hero stood there, listening to her private lion, and to fainter family voices coming up the stairs from below. She imagined her story, leaping up into the sky, shaking its mane of smoke, and then slowly dissolving over the city, becoming not just one but many stories.

At last, she moved back to the computer where the last and only version of her story sat, silver-white on a screen the color of a summer sky.

"Hero! Lunch is on the table," Mike called up the stairs.

With a sigh so deep it was almost a groan, Hero pressed a button on the keyboard. The word-processing program asked her a question.

DELETE? it inquired in white print along the bottom of the screen. CONFIRM Y/N?

Hero pressed the "Y".

For a second nothing happened. Then the words suddenly vanished from the screen, leaving nothing but blueness. Though she had often seen this happen, Hero jumped a little, startled by the sudden disappearance. Her story was gone—told and gone. It would never be found again. Hero stared solemnly into the blue, then slowly began to smile, welcoming her old friend silence once more, silence reinvented, repossessed and magical.

"Hey!" said a voice. Sammy stood in the doorway. "Your family! What a crew! But I reckon your old man means it. No closet kids in *this* house. Slam-dunk!" He saw her staring at the blank screen. "I thought you'd finished with all that."

"I have," said Hero.

"You've worked out what it was about?" asked Sammy.

"Sort of," Hero replied, smiling. "I wrote a whole book."

"Right on!" said Sammy. "That's *w-r-i-t-e* on," he added. "See? I'm catching the Rapper family sickness. I'll be a reject-man."

"It's not just us," said Hero. "It's words themselves. They

were making you itch, reject-man, long before you stopped off here."

Sammy came up behind her.

"So . . . ?" he asked her, and ran his finger down the back of her neck. Hero felt the breath she was taking stop halfway. She lost power over it, abandoned it, and went on to the next one.

"Just sitting! Sitting and listening!"

"Listening?" he asked. "There's nothing to hear. Snap out of it. Let's get weaving."

As he spoke, from somewhere far beyond him, Hero heard the trace of a cry. The roar of the fire, busily feeding behind her, swallowed the sound, but it was not an imaginary echo of Jorinda Credence's screams. It was the experimental wail of a distant chain saw. As she rose, Hero glanced briefly through the long window across other Benallan roofs to the green line of the Credence forest. She thought once more of Miss Credence, who had continued Jorinda's story with a story of her own . . . a story through which real happenings twisted like dark serpents winding through a garden. Hero thought she could see the forest tremble, as once, standing at its dappled edges, she had trembled, too.

Sammy began to dance beside her.

"Stop that writing, listening, blinking . . .
There's more to life than merely thinking,
Come down now 'cause it's time for lunch
Then we'll run, run, run! Keep ahead of the bunch!
Let's you and me rap out of this story
And dazzle the world with a different glory."

"OK, but lunch first," said Hero. Then she turned the computer off, and they clattered downstairs together.

"Where are you two off to?" Mike asked, so carelessly that everyone knew he was listening keenly for the answer.

"Hey," said Sammy. "What's the big worry? You think she might get me pregnant?"

"That's enough of that!" exclaimed Ginevra, looking startled.

"Aha!" Annie said to her triumphantly. "Just you wait until you find how *difficult* it all is."

"She's old enough to have a *boyfriend*," cried Sap. "I've got two . . . both hunky guys." She rolled her eyes and grinned.

Hero looked at Sammy.

"He's safe with me," she said quickly. "Anyhow, he said lunch was ready."

"It's only soup," Mike said. "But what soup! Grab a bowl each, and help yourselves."

So they both grabbed bowls.

"We're going to run round the park a few times," Sammy explained to Mike in a conciliatory voice. "We're going to get really fit, and go in for that great All-Comers Winter Race on Queen's Birthday weekend."

"All this running!" said Mike, smiling and shaking his head.

"It's great," Sammy told him. "If you've got a bit of pace, then you really can keep way out in front of the bunch. No one can touch you, man."

And a little later, Sammy and Hero jogged off side by side, down Edwin Street, leaving the fire in the stove upstairs to finish its feast, and to find, on the other side of that feast, a silence of its own.